DEVINE

J.R. TILMAN

Acknowledgments

First and foremost I want to thank my Mommy, Sonya Adams for everything! When I first got out on my own I was in a completely different state. I pushed to have everything I needed but when it got too much for me I gave it all to Jehovah and my mother came through for me.

I want to especially thank my sister, Shauntia Tilman for her idea to branch out my horizon and open my mind to writing another kind of genre.

I want to thank my Dad, Rodney Tilman, for always being there for me with motivation and keeping my optimism on the rise each time I thought about giving up.

I want to thank my best friends, Tatiana Fears, Caleb Weaver, and Eric Briggs-Claypool for being there for me every step of the way and giving me advice throughout my entire journey!

Dedication

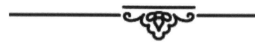

I want to dedicate this book and any other work that I complete in this life to Jehovah! The Lord, my God is my shepherd. Jesus thought I was important enough to die for, and I will never live in vain.

Contents

Chapter 1

Sustainability

"Uhh! Uhh!"

First thing that came to mind was how good this chic's face looks from the back. I could tell all she wanted was a piece of this dark chocolate dick to melt inside of this fat ass pussy from the first time we locked eyes. And I was giving it to her. I mean shit, who wouldn't want to break down a fine ass light bright face who basically threw herself at a niggah? Besides all the bullshit that comes with having good dick I think she understands that it comes with a price. One that doesn't have anything to do with me of course.

"Harder! Uhh! Devine! Devine!" She yells.

I'm panting back to back, "damn baby you leaking all over my sheets...fuck!"

Almost half an hour in and my lungs damn near collapse trying to handle this big ass booty. *Shit!* The faster I pump the more air escapes me. And the harder her fat ass cheeks clap against my thighs.

"Ouu! Don't stop! I'm about to cum daddy! Ahh!"

1

Damn, I be so gone sometimes my mind just drifts off into a deep ass abyss or something.

"Ahh! Stop! Get off of me!

"Trisha!" I yelled. "Get the fuck off her!"

My body froze in the threshold. At that point in time I couldn't think of a single thing that could save her from the gang of men surrounding her and smushing her frail body into the bed.

"Devine. Devine!"

My head shook in a hard circle, "huh? What girl?"

Our bodies collide into the bed.

"Damn girl, what's up?"

"You!" She snarks, "last time I checked my name was Keisha, and you sitting here calling me some trick named Trisha! I know my pussy good as hell but you in here daydreaming about another bitch..."

"Baby, I swear that's not what I meant to say!"

Jumping up from the bed, "oh right because you're not only a lying piece of shit," throwing her clothes on, "you fucking nutted all over my back."

"Huh?"

Her fine ass was right. My fingertips were so deep into the sheets that I could've ripped the silk off them. My thoughts were more corrupt than most survivors of war. I mean that was one thing I couldn't help.

"Fuck you nigga!"

I wrapped the sheets around my body and leapt in front of the door.

I can see a few tears smearing her makeup. Then I thought. *Why would she wear makeup like I wasn't going to go ham in that shit?* Then I answered my own question with a question: *Maybe we moved too fast?* If we took the time out to learn more than each other's last names I wouldn't be huddling against the door literally holding my dick in my hand.

"Wait, wait, wait, wait baby it's really not even like that!" Gripping her waist, "I assure you it's not."

"Yeah right!" She snarked back, "that big ass nut you just bussed when you spaced out says otherwise."

Fuck. My mind drifted off again. I guarantee when she walks out that door she'll have my ass tomorrow. *Good thinking bro.* Worrying about some pussy instead of what really matters. Better yet, I needed my ass whooped. Either way she tucked her shirt back into her skirt faster than a fat kid eating cake.

Her little voice screeched out loud as hell, "and you know what? I was thinking about sparing you tomorrow but I'm going to do your ass in, and after that you'd be lucky if your office sees another case in the state of California again!"

"Damn it's like that baby?"

"Yeah, she paused, it is."

I took a few steps back, tugging on my beard while I glared into her pretty ass brown eyes.

"Look", lowering my voice, "I know we went straight in but you're more than just a fuck to me," gripping my hands around her waist, "you got your head on straight, take care of your kids, on top of your slim waist, pretty face. Woo!"

"Oh shut up," red circles formed on her cheeks, "you lucky you are fine as hell... because I was going to ruin your career tomorrow."

She was right about one thing. I had her mind in this bedroom but in the field she is one bad muthafucka. It would've been like fighting a piranha on steroids. Good thing I have a better mouthpiece than a nigga on his way to jail. I almost thought I lost her.

Anyways if she was going to stick around a fine man like myself she would have to put up with all the 'me' time I need, plus I like to disappear from this fucked up world we live in from time to time. You see more bullshit in the news and media than on the streets of Los Angeles. I take pride in doing my part to make the world a better place. I think of it as a fantastic way to pay my debt to society.

Flopping down on the bed, "tell me one thing," her lips purred. "and I will leave it alone and you never have to speak on it again."

"And what's that?"

"Tell me who Trisha is?"

"Well, she... she..."

"Come on niggah spit it out you know how to talk."

My eyes twisted on every wall in the room, thirsty to find one reason to throw her off the answers she's searching for. One thing I learned in life was allowing people to be all up in your business caused drama. A lot of it at that.

"Babe, I don't think that's... she's nobody."

Keisha's eyelashes flapped faster than her lips moved. "And you know what? You think just because you make a decent amount of money, live in this uppity ass neighborhood, you can do whatever you want, well woo!" mocking my voice, "I'm on your ass tomorrow."

Snatching her purse off the nightstand she stomps out of my bedroom door, almost knocking every picture I had of me pinned on the wall down.

I stretch out on my bed. My eyes couldn't help but watch the ceiling fan twist in circles.

Fuck, fuck fuck! If I didn't think my career was fucked before I know for a fact that the consequences of her walking out that door with a sad face ended it tonight. I just hope I satisfied her 'girl' more than I did her mind. I figure if I did that she would think about me pounding that shit out before stomping my pride into the ground. She doesn't seem naive one bit but when you get a person alone you can tell if they are faking confidence. All you have to do is listen to their story.

Let's face it. You ever wanted to live a completely different life. Then you find out everything you always thought was true was wrong as fuck. You try to be as authentic as you can, but that shit doesn't get you anywhere because the stress of paying the bills fucks your mind. People want what they want. And if we're being real with one another that's a fantasy. The fantasy of a better life. A fairytale between real life and false dreams. Some people lie to themselves instead of appreciating what they already have. Not many want to treasure their shit until they get to where they want to be. Only the rare. That about sums me up. I give the people the fantasy that they want.

I turn over and smash my head on my pillow.

Even if I told her what she wanted to hear, which was going to be a lie, I would have had to pile one lie on top of the other. I don't need anybody to know my business. And apart from being a 'not shit' niggah to the women I dealt with in the past I never told them lies and I guess that shit didn't help my case either. It happens to be that these bitches love lies more than anything else. They want a muthafucka to dick them down, take them out to eat and tell them whatever they want to hear. Until I start giving this good ass dick to another bitch, then all of a sudden I'm the one with all the secrets and shit. Pshh, whatever hoe, you only care about getting yo hair and nails did in the first place. I know for a fact I'm not the one mistaken either. Unless I attract all the wrong women in my life back to back, I live my life better off alone.

Watching the fan blades I nod off.

Beep! Beep! Beep! Beep!

Damn! What the fuck! A loud ass ding damn near split my ear drums. Turning around to get a quick glance at the clock and it's already half past seven. I get up and hop in the shower to beat the morning traffic. As the warm water hit my skin I think of different ways my life could have turned out. It took more than half of it to get where I am today but man, sometimes it feels like my world changed overnight. And a nigga not going anywhere anytime soon, I pray heavy on that. It be like the more I stay out of the way the more shit drops on my front doorstep. How am I supposed to be if I use each occurrence in my life as a stepping stone that runs straight into another fuckin' problem? I just wanted to get to the bag and get some pussy along the way. I guess I fell inside of the naive pool of hope. The kind that you gravitate to when you make good money you expect your problems to disappear. The biggest fuckin' lie in all of history! Matter of fact, the more money you make the more issues you have to deal with. Especially if you are a Black man in America. Shit. People use that shit as a weapon against you. That's that narcissist shit they play on muthafuckas...throwing stones and hiding their hands when you react just to make it seem like you're the problem. And those were the exact people that I fight to protect my energy from.

Dun dun dun da dun da dun dun!

That might be Alesha! I jump out of the shower to grab my phone because that's a call I can't afford to miss. I look at the screen for a few seconds before I pick it up.

"Man what does this niggah want?" I huff. "Hello Mr. Jeffery," clearing my throat, "what is it that I can help you with today?"

"Yes, hello Mr. Staxx, how are you today?" he continued, "I was calling to let you know that we have found additional evidence on your client, and we are going to offer a deal of 25 years max in court today, but if you wanted..."

"Uhm," cutting him off, "Mr. Jeffrey I am well aware that my client's DNA wasn't discovered on any of the bodies found in the warehouse and that gives the prosecution a very weak defense against my client."

"Oh, yes, I am not inclined to give away any classified information regarding the new evidence that is being presented in the motion of discovery, but I was inclined to give you a call in exchange for a favor on Keisha's behalf."

Pumping my fist through the air, "Uhm-uhm, how sweet of her. However, I am looking to get my client's charges dropped to associating with a criminal gang, so we're looking at 5 years maximum."

Yeah! I knew Keisha had it in her heart to give a niggah a break. She got that act of confidence shit down packed. Good thing I knew what to say to have her ass brainstorming on her ride home. Even with the sex playing a major part she needed a sense of comfort to mend the broken heart she carries around from her father leaving her at such a young age. See, it always helps to be a good listener, women love that shit! After a few shots I just listened to her vent about how heartbreaking it is to always be tossed to the side for someone else. She just happened to be seasoned enough to be aware that life has no favors, only trades. This was the trade I needed!

I felt his wide ass smirk through the phone, "Mhm, I am very aware that you are one of the best lawyers in the city, better yet in the state of California," he said, "but with this new evidence we have I assure you not even you can get these charges dropped to mere gang affiliation. You'd be better off taking this new deal and saving both the court, yourself and the prosecution a headache."

Mr. Jeffery falls into the category of the 'white man' bowing to the 'white man'. Other than his name he acts like one of those cheapskate ass people who tries so hard to impress the King Goblins anyway he can. Shit he probably trying so hard to make himself relevant that he's sucked a million dicks to even be representing anyone on Keisha's side.

"Oh, I am very positive that this witness you came across is obviously a desperate attempt to save your office from the state pulling funding from it. "

Being blindsided by his punk ass attempt of a favor I have to make it my mission to play mind games. Better his than mine. There has to be a better way of getting what I needed from the defense, or I'd be more than fucked.

His breath spoke up louder than his voice.

"And what source do you have to think our funding is under threat Mr. Staxx?"

Got him! People like Mr. Jeffery will ride the bike until the wheels fall off. I can call out all his weaknesses, but one thing he does have is the great skill of patience. Enough to ride this case out on top of fighting for whatever time he sees fit for my client. Both he and I know that my client going down without concrete evidence will never happen with me as his defense.

Giving these white folk an inch clears an automatic mile in their eyes. Staying on your P's and Q's is a must. Rule number one as a black man in America; never give anybody a chance to claim your weakness. That goes especially for the white man. It doesn't take a history major to notice the massive difference between a white man being convicted versus a black man.

If I continue on with this conversation I can ruin my chance of redeeming Keisha's full trust. She might have attempted to 'help' my client, however her qualifications prove damn well she know how the game go, and she knows it well.

Shifting his attention, "any who," I spoke up, "my client is innocent and without solid evidence he will be free by the end of February."

Raising his voice, "uhh-um! I see. Well then, eye for an eye it is!"

The crackle in his throat revealed everything I needed to know to dig deeper.

"Hmh," shrugging my shoulders, "see you in court."

Beep, beep, beep.

Rushing into my closet I throw on the coldest suit I had hanging up. I race to my front door with one thought running through my mind. If I look good I feel good and that means other people think the same. I caught a glimpse of my reflection in the mirror on my way out of the front door. *You that niggah.* I say to myself. Here we go. Time to make this money, and time to make it make sense!

Before hopping into my car I stared at the exterior to appreciate it for a few seconds. Anyone who used to know me would swear I couldn't afford a Mercedes Benz. 'Oh he's paying car notes, 'it's his sugar mommy's car', a poor black man spending money on materialistic shit.' Whatever muthafuckas.

I appreciate Keisha's attempt to help out but that fool speaking on her behalf can get her license taken away. Either way that shit was bogus. Any other man probably would run after the opportunity to make a deal with her team. Lucky for me I ain't a regular muthafucka that goes for anything.

Rule number two; 'stand for nothing, fall for anything'. Well that's at least what I used to press my Trisha on all the time.

They say 'time heals all wounds', mhm, yeah right. That's most definitely for the birds. It's been over ten years since I lost my baby girl. And a niggah ain't never been the same. It's like whenever the tides take a turn it's for the worst. We had it so good for so long that we thought our world would never end.

The day Trisha and I first met it felt like the whole world dropped off my back. Everyday I'd wake up and walk right to the store at the corner of my mama's house. Back then I had a strong addiction to Zebra cakes. You know those little white cakes with the

,ocolate frosting lines going up and down across each side. I still grab a pack of those from time to time. Anyways, the owner worked every single day like he never took a day off. With that being said he had my pack of cakes sitting at the front counter waiting on me every single day.

"Aye!" I screeched, "you got my shit right where I like it... front and center!"

"Aww come on Fetch you know how I do?"

Awe man, that niggah Esteban used to crack me the hell up with his little nicknames. Calling me 'Fetch' to over exaggerate how I managed to eat a box of cakes each day and come fetch some more the next. He reminded me of that one dude that played in the movie where he was murkin' shit back to back but took that little girl in to take care of her until he got jammed up fucking with that obsessed ass police officer.

I always wanted an Arab friend. For some reason that movie convinced me that they were very loyal people. Well after my phase of thinking all of them were undercover assassins. To be honest you never know the truth in this turnt out ass world. You see a movie swear it's real life then they turn around and tell you that it's not. At the same time you can't do anything but take it in as that, it's not like you don't have your own life to worry about...

I was used to huffs going on behind my back so the little grunt noises made no difference to how I would carry on with my day. I wallowed side to side laughing at Esteban before handing him over my dollars.

A small voice thumped against my ear drums, "uhm, can you like hurry up?"

I thought about finishing my last sentence before turning around and telling this little dude about himself. Everyone in the hood knew Spade came down to the Corner store for his favorite cakes *every morning. There was no doubt in my mind that it had to be a newcomer who was about to be put in his place real quick.*

Finishing up our conversation I handed over the few dollars I saved up that week. Brainstorming two to three different ways this situation was about to go I took in a steep breath of air. Back then my name rang bells like a ghetto superstar.

"Aye look bro." I paused in mid-sentence.

"Yeah," she spoke up, "I knew you weren't talking to me."

My eyes batted twice as hard when I looked down at her glittered out kicks then back up to her perfectly trimmed short cut.

"What?" She asked, "nothing to say little Fetch?" Her sarcasm spoke softer than her rough voice.

A young dude like me thought that falling in love at first sight was nothing more than some myth they play out in those movies for money. 'Suckers.' Little pussy boys fell in-love with some woman that ran the show, or the 'household. And before you knew it I fell right into the category of one of those little 'pussy's'. Just so happened that I very much loved being one of those coochie boys. I swear she put some kind of spell on a nigga that made me want to change my entire world or some shit. It was like I saw my life change right in the middle of those hazel eyes of hers.

Struggling to get a single word out. "Oh, I...I,"

"Cat got your tongue?"

"I think I love you."

"Ahh! Ha! Ha!" Esteban's hooting and hollering went in one ear and out of the other.

Her pink lips stretched to both her ears.

That was it for me. That day was the first day of the rest of our lives. Whoever would have thought young 'Spade' would be all up somebody's daughter's ass. Most times I wish she never ran into me at the store that day. Sometimes I wish I never even met

:r at all. When the past can't come back and bite you in the ass, t never left. That's when you are certain that your mind is fucked. I always knew better but it seemed like every which way I turned, doing better wasn't in my dictionary.

"Mr. Staxx. Mr. Staxx."

I shake my head. "Huh, what?"

I made it to the office already? *Damn*. In a minute I may need to hit up Sasha again for a few of those top notch therapy sessions. Only if she promises to be on her best behavior this time and not cutting up all my shit. I had to reinvest in an entire wardrobe last time I spoke to her.

"Are you okay?" Alesha asked. "I saw you sitting outside for a few minutes and wanted to see if you were okay?"

"Yes, yes, I'm fine," tugging the buttons on my suit, "what we got?"

We walk over to the building damn near clutched to each other's side.

"Wait, wait, wait," I slide over, "what did I tell you about practicing professionalism while we're at work?"

Her eyes open wide as hell, "and what did I tell you about not slinging dick around the whole city?"

This bitch is crazy. Alesha is the kind of hoe that'll get you jammed up whenever you tell her ass no. Why out of all of the pussy she tossing around she wants to give me the most problems. It ain't like she not fucking the whole office. On top of that she giving it to half the old white dudes who have wives at home. She not gone fool me with the okie doke. Wanting to give out migraines for no reason.

Easing closer to her, "look," I lower my voice, "I already told you what we had is over, understand?"

Our eyes lock tighter.

Shrugging her shoulders, "oh, I know that" she laughs, "I was just coming to give you a few pointers."

"And what's that on? Getting the help you need instead of crying for it with open legs."

"No nigga. Try not fucking the competition when your back is up against the wall."

Oh! She is trying the fuck outta me. That goes to show that exercising my rules topped out even the number one rule. People will always try to get a reaction out of the fear you hold on too. If I even bat an eye at her assumption she will think she won the battle. *Nah.* Devine don't lay down at nobody's feet.

"Look Miss. Winder, you are a very bright young woman and an amazing assistant," I went on, "but we both know that we were feeling ourselves a couple times off the Quavo, and we made some mistakes."

She got quiet for a few seconds, "but you told me you loved me," her voice crackled, "you told me you cared about me."

Chapter 2

What's Authority?

"**A**nd little baby I do," stroking her arm, "but, still, you are a little too young for me and I know you don't want a complicated old dude like me."

I had no business diving deep into her ocean the way I did. At the same time she wouldn't let up either. You can tell a woman how it's going to be up front, in the beginning they all cool with seeing what it's hittin' for, then next they breaking in your house and tearing up all your shit. And not the quick pick outfits you grab when you out at JCPenney, but the Dolce and Gabbana gear you get at the outlets. I thought dealing with different people after changing your surroundings came with better results.

That's the problem these days with these women. You give them all the right attention and they don't appreciate that shit until it's gone. For sure I thought I wanted to be with Alesha once upon a time, but that stiff ass attitude matched those wigs she was wearing. The second she started throwing out all kinds of demands like a niggah balling out of control. Well I am that niggah. And I'm balling out of control. But still, she also has a lot of anger she needs to put at bay. More issues than I can deal with.

Her fingernails pat under both her eyelids, "so this is what you do right?" She asked, "you fuck me then you take one of the biggest snake lawyers in the city out for drinks and home?"

"What?" I yank down on her dress, "you've been following me? Again?!"

Man, I swear these women don't get enough of crashing out on me. No doubt that Alesha is more than a ten, especially when she actually has all that beautiful natural hair draping down to her fat ass. I love me a pure dark chocolate woman. Matter of fact I adore all kinds of women. Short, tall, thick, slim, light, dark, mixed, white. I can't get enough of the cookies they tossed into my bed. And dawg were they sweet cookies.

I lower my voice.

"You have no business following me and if you do it again I will have your ass out of here in the blink of an eye."

"Oh yeah, and how are you going to do that? Huh?" She snaps back, "what's your excuse going to be?"

Glaring down at my wristwatch and the time flew past my first meeting time. See what I'm talking about? Got a niggah all mixed the fuck up. She so worried about herself that she didn't remind me of it.

"Mhm, just have my coffee on my desk in a few minutes."

Backing up from this trick before I have her ass laying out on the street somewhere is the best thing for me to do right now. There is no telling how long she's been stalking me around again instead of doing her job. How hard is it for people to get with the program before they get left behind? All she has to do is be on time and drop a cup of coffee off on my desk. *Pshh.* I wish I had her job; she don't have to be in the field everyday dealing with bum ass prosecutors, slimy ass lawyers, or worked over convicts. I most definitely empathize that her father left her mother to fend for her at a young age, but she turned out fine to me. She, like everybody else's pappy who dipped on they ass, has some built up trauma. That don't mean she can run around blaming it on everybody else. You don't see me crying wolf about my sorry ass pops. My momma should have left that nigga more than ten years before she did. Fuck it though, old habits seem to never die. And that's something she's going to have to learn quick.

I walk in the building with my eyes straight forward.

"Hey glad you made it in, we have great news to share about the..."

"Put it on my desk."

"Hey, there has been a breaking news report that has exposed some very disturbing news about one of our clients."

"Alert Alesha," I reply.

All the rambling in the world can't stop me from floating into my office. I am tired of these people with their ass goofy behavior. My focus has to be at its greatest for this trial today. My assistant is lame as hell, and I hopped in bed with this broad for nothing...well at least some good pussy came out of that. Still, shit was so kosher a before this case came flopping down on my desk. These folks ain't gone to take me out the game though. If anything, I'm a soldier to this shit.

Knock. Knock.

"What is it?" I ask.

I sit behind my desk praying to stay calm for a few minutes. Just one second... one, to calm the raging thoughts taking over the space in my mind.

"Uhh-um, it's Tristian Sir," he announces himself.

"Come in."

Making his way through my door he starts talking but I can't help to notice all that damn cologne burning up my nose hairs.

"What is it Tristian?"

Shutting the door behind his back, "so sorry to bother you," his breath is hazy, "but we may have a major problem with your primary case."

Fucking great. Like I said, one problem after another. Burning this muthafucka down to the ground didn't sound too bad right now. I always try to think about the reason I got into this field of work in the first place? At the time I figured the best way to protect myself from the devils was to learn every way of the law. Better to beat them rather than join them.

You know how it feels when you first conquer a great challenge you never thought you could? I remember when I enjoyed being a lawyer. Helping all the young bros' fight cases in the joint. Every Saturday morning I'd be the last one to make my way out of the law's library. Well, at least when they gave us the chance to learn something in that bitch. Busting knives through each other's chest felt more like a regular day than picking up a book.

I always had a hard time accepting that the facts of life were simple. My granny made it seem like you either go to school, work a job or you'd be doomed. Sometimes I wish I went for the typical life my mom fought for me to have. Wife, nine to five, dream home for my kids to come to anytime the world steps on their toes. But then reality sets in. I'd have to get up every day and go to someone's factory, cater to somebody else's needs twenty four seven, and may even struggle to pay my bills to keep my life afloat. Struggle comes with chasing dreams, and completing the goal doesn't mean the struggle is over. It has only just begun. That's what most people don't realize.

"So sorry about that," Tristian said, "if we knew that sooner we would have..."

"Wait," I cut in, "knew what?"

The red circles popping up on both sides of his face told me some kind of disappointing news is coming.

"Excuse me Sir I thought you heard me say that we lost the request for getting Javeon's bond."

"Yes... I'm aware that our argument was not going to stick due to lack of evidence to support it."

"Yes, and uhm..."

His eyes circled around the room. Making my heart bang against my chest a little harder than usual.

"What is it?" I ask.

Damn. What now? Who knew that me agreeing to play Mr. Nice and Sane 'Guy' with all the answers would be a major burden. It seems that everybody wants a piece of what I worked hard as hell for. Between the courts, prosecutors, and judges, it all seems to be a constant thing. A crumbled cycle of power no one really has.

"Well Sir I know the company policy stresses how important it is to be 100 percent legit, so the opposing side has no advantages over us and... and."

Smashing my teeth down on my lip, "come on now spit it out," I cut in, "whatever it is I'm sure it isn't the end of the world."

"Well, I have an inside source that is telling me the prosecution has solid evidence that places your client's fingerprints on the weapon that killed Officer Miles at the warehouse."

"And where did this evidence come from?"

"They stated that they have a solid witness who can not only place Javeon at the warehouse but that indeed he is the Kingpin of the entire Hotboyz Corporation."

I feel like I can blow a gasket and bust all the blood out of my skull right now. I been all over this case for months. Two questions in the air, who in the possible hell could this witness be? And why the fuck is the prosecution taking all fucking year to hand over the motion of discovery, I guess Keisha was wrong. I'm going to have her ass along with her gremlin ass partner in court! Then I'm going to ask to take her out to dinner afterwards. You know, to let her know who the real brain in this situation is.

Raising up from my chair, "no matter what," my eyes staring into his, "whatever you are doing with whoever on the prosecutor's team..."

"I'm so sorry boss," he cut in, "I know you are a man of integrity and I look up to you so much for this but..."

"No," I took a quick pause, "keep doing it."

Clearing my throat breaks the dead silence between the two of us. Although Tristian is right to look up to my honorable ways when doing business, this matter has to be dealt with accordingly. There is no way I can lose this case to Keisha's team.

With the importance of this case the least I can do is pretend I didn't just hear one of my star pupils admit to fucking one of our competitors, shit, I guess Apple don't fall too far from the tree. I can dig deeper but I won't. Even him giving me the heads up helps in the opportunity to tear these muthafuckas apart..

"Well, okay, go out there and get my afternoon file ready for trial."

"About that Sir," his voice lowers, "your client has also demanded that you see him before court."

"What do you mean? Demanded?"

Tristian is one of those young cats who grew up in the suburbs. Black Dad, White Momma, so he be acting all scary to speak and shit.

"Didn't I tell you to contact me immediately if that certain client makes any kind of demands?"

"Yes, but..."

Every word coming out of his big ass lips went in one ear and out of the other. The one thing I know I can't afford is one of my biggest paying clients making it his mission to look for other representation. Which I know he won't, still Tristian knows I put in work day in and day out to get this case over with a W. He always cries about being on computer duty, but he can't even do his job right. Who has a problem with getting twenty dollars an hour to pick up a damn phone? These young people these days man...

If I rise up from my desk I know he is going to shit his pants. I find it best that I hold onto the tad bit of composure of not knocking this little niggah on his ass. We all know a pretty boy; light skin marks don't heal well.

Clearing my throat, "look, I have certain rules in place to make sure that this place runs a certain way," I say, "and that allows all of our pockets to stay filled along with no complication."

"Yes Sir but I..."

"Which means," I continue, "we all have a part to play. Now when I tell you to make sure you call my phone even if you hear a burp come out the mouth of Javeon McCleaton you dial me on the phone. Understand?"

"I'm so sorry Sir, it will never happen again."

Clank!

What the fuck?! Ugh! Here comes this bimbo ass broad bustin' through my door like the swat team on a Sunday morning. If she keeps showing her ass in my place of business I'm going to drag her ass out both of those doors by those thin ass heels she prances around in! Shawty damn near knocked Tristian to the floor face first.

"Uh-uhm," I get up, "is there something wrong with your knuckles that you can't knock on my door before entering?"

20

Both her eyes do a quick twist, "I have information that is more important than you two in a dick holding contest."

Moms always taught me to respect the shit out of women but the audacity of this little bitch! To check me outside of my establishment is one thing, trying to embarrass me in front of one of my rising workers is what's going to get her ass up out of here. Quick!

"Tristian," exhaling a steep breath, "go clear my voicemails and tell my nine a.m. that I apologize, and we need to reschedule."

"Yes Sir," he says."

The way he bolts out of the door makes it clear he knows what's going on. I'm pretty sure he is also aware of her smashing record right along with the rest of the office.

"Aye look girl, you can't be busting all up in my office like we fuckin'."

Okay. Okay. I admit it. I fucked up by sticking dick into my assistant. She don't give a fuck about none of my rules either, but at the same time that crazy shit makes me want to bend her ass over on this desk and squeeze my hand over her mouth. Some men prefer their women to be all extra obedient, me? I like a little frisk in females, it show me she ain't the one to be played with. I thought Alesha carried this trait in her, she proved that theory wrong months ago. I just figured that she has no right to care about me if she is doing her too.

I sit back down in my chair forcing the twitch in my eyebrow away.

"Mhm," she mumbles, "are you turned on daddy?"

After twisting the blinds shut she flips the lock on my door.

Fuck no! Devine don't do it bro! The screaming in my head disappears the second she flips her hand then shoves it up her dress.

"Damn baby you're just going to play with that little shit right in front of me?" Licking one of her fingers, she put the other one on the tip of my bottom lip.

"You know you want it baby?"

She drops down on my lap dragging her tongue across my neck got me feeling some kind of way with the quickness.

"Sheesh!" I grumble. "You just like to take shit, huh?"

"Yup baby," she continues to suck on my neck, "and this is how I'm going to do your dick next."

Is this how it's gonna be? Have thots suck the veins on my dick in my place of business. I complained about everything, and reputation is one of the many. The thought of losing this place over community pussy is beyond crazy but I can't stop Jack from the great rise he gets every time she is around me. Alesha has one of those water park pussy's. That one kind that keeps leaking from the moment it starts.

"Shit," whispering in her ear, "I'm going to tear that fat shit up."

"Mhm daddy," moaning back, "and tell me how much that other bitch pussy ain't better than mine."

This is where most women blow the tiny shot they think they have with me. I'm already kind enough to bless you with all this dick and you have the nerve to speak on the next. It is my fault for sure. To think after ten minutes of this young woman with the sense of an adolescent with zero respect for the man who keeps her bills paid every month, has an ounce of respect for herself? Hell nah. Instead she's so worried about the other bitch I'm knocking down that she doesn't care what happens to her.

Sitting up in my chair, "see this is where we're going to end this." I say, "get up... get up off me."

"Huh," her eyes are bulk, "what do you mean get off of you?!"

"Shh," the veins in my throat thump against my neck, "if you ever think I will fuck yo' little thot ass where I make my money you mistook me for another niggah."

Pushing her to her feet, our glares have no effect on the amount of power banging up against my chest. This little hoe thinks she can play me like I'm one of these rookie white folks running after her. She crossed the line once she chose to show up at my spot unannounced, now she thinks it's okay to bust in my office. *Nah.* She, like everybody else got me fucked up. But she gone learn just who she fucking with today.

"Fuck you muthafucka!" her loud ass mouth hollered on, "you think you foolin' everybody, but I figured out who you really are!"

And the real her comes to life...

Twisting my wristwatch, "bitch you don't know shit about me," I look at the door, "now you can see your way out my shit before I drag you out myself."

With the veins popping through her skull I can tell she thinks givin' up her pussy is the answer to all her problems. Maybe she can get away with that energy with one of those bird brains but not over here. Today she's going to remember who runs all this shit.

"Mhm," she smirks, "stop bluffing', you're just another sorry ass hood nigga tryna cover it up with proper white people talk and nice suits."

"Ha," I smirk right back, "I don't even disrespect women, I know better than that so I'm going to let you walk out of here with the little piece of dignity you have left..."

"Bitch shut up!" She screams, "you knew what you was getting yourself into the second you jumped in bed with me."

Looking towards the door, "guards get Miss. Tucker out of here!"

I mean... this is what I get. I need to stop letting Jack control both my heads. Out of all the commotion her weak ass was going on about she is right about one thing. I am from the streets, the dirty up North ghetto dirty dawg trenches. Still I never forgot how I made it out of Toledo with my head held higher than a muthafucka. On top of me being fresh as fuck I remained the best to ever do it!

I handle my own, that means one hundred percent no disrespect from anyone.

She is more than lucky I keep security on hand in the office. Sadly she isn't the only trick who likes to pop up out the blue and disrupt my space. One day these rat hoes are going to learn when to separate drama from the bag, that or to keep their funky ass legs closed to keep feelings in check.

"Stop!" Yanking away from security, "ouu! I promise this isn't the last time you're going to see me!"

She went on and on.

"Gentlemen please escort this young woman off the premises." I say calmly.

"You're a fake ass nigga! And I'm going to let everybody with open ears know who you really are! Ace!"

My eyes damn near popping out of both my sockets, forcing the air to settle down from hammering up against my chest.

I shut the door behind them.

My homeboy Drew hard-pressed on the controller.

"Yo Ace bro! You cheating man."

We used to sit up all day making plays, juggin', and late at night bet on who got the master bedroom to break off one of those bad shawties we picked up along the ride.

"Aye niggah!" I laughed, "I'm gonna win this bet, and tonight looks like I'm relaxing in a king size bed."

"Man shut yo' proper sounding ass up," he mocked my voice, "I'm going to 'relax' tonight... get outta' here!"

I can say even with me damn near being homeless for two years after I got out the pin in some weird way I made a home with the gang. Drew never made me out to be this big bad guy the rest of the city painted in their heads. I never knew if he just accepted me for who I was because he was worse than me or he just didn't give a fuck.

"Aye yo', pass the wood Drop," Drew called across the room, "you acting like you just so clutch with rollin' but take all fucking day."

Cutting in front of the flat screen, "aye bruh all you do is cry all day like a brat," Drop passed Drew the blunt, "you act worse than the hoes."

"Aye bro move, you're blocking my view," I said.

"Man," Drop pointed at me, "Drew where'd you find this niggah' man sound like he been studying the dictionary all his life."

Chapter 3

Growing Pains

"**M**hm," sucking my teeth, "nah bruh, don't worry about my proper etiquette," raising up from the chair, "you just sit over there, and roll blunts because we know who brings the most money in this joint."

"Yo both of y'all need to chill the fuck out," Drew jumped in between us, "I know yo' temper short as hell and you don't need to catch another fuckin' case after a five year bid bro," he looked at me then Drop, "and you still need to go the store and get my menthol's."

Our eyes locked for only a few more seconds until he realized that I wasn't that one to play with for real. Back then most muthafuckas I stomped out thought me knowing how to articulate my words made me soft. It was during my time I showed my true colors in Ross jail. After choking a few folks 'til they passed out, word spread fast as hell to stay out my way. And I loved every second of it. Better them than me. Right?

"Man it's twelve other niggahs cooped up in this little ass apartment why do I always have to make the store runs Drew?"

Drew tugged on his shirt collar, "because muthafucka," his voice got lower, "my fiend, my house, and you not bringing us no licks to hit, no pills to serve, you don't even have hoes niggah." Releasing him, "So you lucky I don't fuck yo' burnt ass up myself."

"Yeah aight," Drop backed up.

He stomped out the door.

If I didn't learn anything from living with a bunch of dudes for five years straight it's the amount of respect you get from holding your own. That little twitch in your eye lids spoke more than any words could say. Most times your opposition tested the power of force you had just by the strength in your eyes. Me? I carried all the weight the world offered in my eyes, no pain could have creeped inside my aura or on my shoulders.

Drew and I continued to focus on the Xbox.

"Aye bro," he said, "I know you fresh out a couple of months, but I haven't heard you say anything about yo' moms since you came back from yo' granny crib."

Breathing out a quick breath, "well I don't think my personal life is none of your business," I replied.

"Hold on bro," dropping the controller, "when we were in the joint bustin' heads together you were this open ass book, now you want to be all up tight and shit," he said, "don't think I didn't notice your whole attitude change after you came back yesterday."

Drew was the type of dude to wear his heart on his sleeve. Don't get it twisted he still hemmed niggahs up as much as I did. We found common ground and ended up creating a bond before his sentence got cut short and he got released early for good behavior. Which only meant everybody knew not to snitch on us or the consequences would be rough.

Before God gave me a second chance after my life was nearly snatched away from me, Drew made my first time in the joint more easy. He was like the brother I never had. But I didn't look forward to speaking on my 'mommy' issues. Especially after not hearing anything from her my whole bid.

I was so alone in the pen I damn near told him my whole life story. It was uncanny how much we had in common. Like we both had cracked out moms, the only difference is that his happened to leave him in the garbage can at birth. My OG wasn't always like the fiends I served. She tried to raise me to be a suitable young man up until she had enough of Pops beating her upside the head every single night. After some time, we managed to make it out and after she dropped me off on her momma's front porch my life changed forever. My granny wasn't one to play with, Ma', was what me and five of my little cousins called her. Beyond being just another motherless child, I became the eldest orphan, which meant I had weight to carry. From Ma's point of view that meant easy shifts between the both of us and her prescription of Perc thirties'.

No big deal though. She made it clear that we were going to be just fine if we always stuck to the plan. When I'm not in the books I make sure old heads are getting their medicine. That was before my short shifts of serving her friends her prescription pills turned into me serving base heads thirty ounces on the corner. By the age 15, I was the most popular corner boy on the South-side of Toledo. My huge ego played better than Beyonce's song. I was clean as hell, happy and loved by the hoes... Well, at least until I ran into Trisha at the store that day. After that no female could pay to get my attention.

"Huh," I sighed, "she wasn't there when I went over there."

"What?" He asked, "well where is she?"

I paused, "when I went over to the corner store across the street from her house Esteban said she died a few years ago."

He got quiet for a minute, "oh damn bro, I'm sorry to hear that. I mean you know you can stay here as long as you need."

His fiend cut in on our conversation.

"Daddy I need some more of that good stuff."

"Aye bitch!" He yelled. "Didn't I tell you when I'm playing the game in my free time you don't talk to me."

Aww man. He treated that poor lady Mable so badly in her own house I almost felt for her. She was so coked out that her mind wouldn't let her care about anything but the next time she got another fix.

He raised up from the chair, "well I got some for you, but you know what you gotta do for it."

"You know I'll suck yo' dick daddy."

Ugh! I didn't care nothing about what he did on his time as long as I had somewhere to lay my head. Although it was a two bedroom apartment with almost ten other people cooped up, it felt better to be there than a cold cell with a hard cot.

Twelve years ago I viewed life in a totally different light. Slumming it up with the bros', getting money, serving and slanging drugs happened to be my way of living my best life. Everyone around me knew not to say shit to me or they'd be under a ditch crying for mommy to come to their rescue.

Knock. Knock.

"Sir, your car is here." Tristian sat at the door.

"Uhh-uhm, coming out now,"

I tug on my collar and tighten the cuff on my suit.

"Let's ride," I open the door.

"Me?" He asks, "you want me to come with you to the court house?"

"Yes, young brother. I think you have paid your desk dues and if you prove that you can handle yourself today there may even be a new assistant position with your name on it."

I try not to keep my head in the clouds about the fact that Alesha knew the name I ran with over a decade ago. There's no way she should have a clue, and now she officially a major problem that needs to be dealt with. No one in this entire state has ever approached me with that name. It died a long time ago with the person I used to be. Even if she did her homework, she knows something I can never afford to get out, no doubt I'll see her later.

We head for the front door. As I ignore the quiet glances from a few of the other lawyers, they know if they stare too long it'll be an unaffordable consequence. Not from me of course but their wives back at the crib. Most of them are great at minding their own business, some were kind of upset that the only play they received got dismissed from the job. In my defense she should have been gone more than a few months ago. The first time she popped up at my crib whining about her baby daddy issues made me feel for her. I never wanted to take away her only income that feeds her son. That just goes to show you can give an ungrateful person your last two cents and they'll demand five more.

"Good morning Mr. Braxter, Sir," my driver says, "two today?"

"Yes," I keep it short, "get in Tristian."

"Oh, yes Sir."

He hops in. In the process of flames damn near bustin' out both my ears I manage to calm it with laughter. This dude Tristian acts so frail it cracks me up every time. I remember my days of being so dingy back then that I got myself into unshakable situations, so I understand what he's going through mentally. I salute him for taking the courage to chase his dreams so early.

We take off from the building.

Sitting in silence for a few minutes I search through my phone to delete Alesha's message thread. Better yet, a brand new phone will be better than this iPhone 10 anyways. I don't want any evidence of our conversation to ever resurface.

The driver asks. "Any extra stops today Sir?"

I lean back against the leather seat, "yes, the phone store right after court will be fine. Thank you."

"Not a problem Sir."

I toss my phone on the seat.

"So, how long before you graduate law school?"

"Well, uhm, 2 more years Sir."

"That's really good to hear. Do you like it?"

"So far so good Sir."

The silence takes over as he grabs on the seatbelt.

"Are you okay?" I ask.

His eyes stare at all the big buildings we pass as we head downtown.

"So sorry Sir... I just never experienced riding inside of a Benz before, now I'm being escorted in one with a person of great stature, it's kind of a dream come true."

This kid is hilarious. I remember my first time riding in a nice car too. I thought I'd never get the chance to see all the cool whips I dreamed of having when I was his age. From running the streets since I came out the womb to having millions of dollars in the bank just didn't add up for a person like me. You don't really see Benz's or Escalade's in the trenches. Only slab's sitting on high ass gold rims or spinners. For a minute your head gets stuck in the ghetto mindset. The thoughts that tell you to sell as much dope as you can to survive or if you get rid of this many pills it will set you up for the rest of your life. Like the justice system, all that shit is a set up. If they told you in school that you need to find the path that lights up your heart to live your best life, most old ass adults wouldn't be strung out on all those prescriptions, and the next generation wouldn't be committing suicide. It's only a matter of time before more people start waking up, but with the way times are now there's no secret that won't be for a while.

"We've arrived Sir," my driver opens the door.

"Go ahead," I look at Tristian.

We both jump out of the car. Tristian looks confused like he never saw downtown before. In a way I find it interesting to show a young buck the game. If he proves he can hang with the big dogs no doubt I got him for the startup of his career. He has proved himself enough at the office for the last three years. If a bimbo like Alesha can handle the snakes in the grass I'm sure he can too. He just has to grow some balls and leave that weak shit at the house every morning. We cut from different cloths for sure but that doesn't mean he never felt pain. I would be a blind fool if I ignored it. In fact every smart man knows first that the pain is what builds you, shaping you into who you are. Also his ass is on the light skinned side which means he still qualifies as a black man in America.

"Wow, look at this scenery," his eyes looks up into the air.

We step into the building passing the security to get on the elevator.

John speaks up, "good morning Mr. Braxter, floor 8 I presume."

"No, heading up to the central holding area," I nod.

One thing I can't stand about most of the lawyers I run across in the field is the fact that they act all uppity and shit like they just have everything figured out in life. Yeah right, most of them muthafuckas barely have a law degree because Paw Paw had a friend at whatever school they graduated from. Like this snake John, his father is one of the biggest investors for the Southern California Institute of Law. Good thing I make it my mission to do my research on any lawyer I face off with in court. I tore him a new ass hole a while back. It taught him an important lesson about not throwing jabs at my intelligence because of the color of my skin. All that, 'this man is not equipped shit' flew out the window the second I got my hands on that dirty ass cop's police footage. For a while it made me mad as hell that I had to study my ass off in the law library in jail then come out and go to school for another seven years just to get my damn law degree. I learned to look at it as I fought my way to greatness, and that's why I be tearin' they ass up in court. They don't understand how a 'bum' ass black man has the knowledge I do. But I'm here to tell you a secret about success, you never wait for it to come, you go get that shit no matter the cost because white boys like John and Brian already have their way paved for them. That shit didn't do anything but make me better at my job.

"Well isn't that where the prisoners are held before court Sir?" Tristian chimes in.

I keep my head facing the door, "yes, but our client requested to see me remember?"

"But lawyers can't go back there, I thought," he replies.

"Let's just say I'm not like any other lawyer."

I throw a small smirk in return to John's side eye. No one can make me feel bad about the pride I carry. Not after all the hell I traveled through to get here.

Ding.

"Come on," I tug on Tristian's sleeve, "we have a client to serve."

We make it up to the guards station where all the inmates are held.

"I'm here to see Javeon McCleaton."

"Lawyers aren't allowed back here," stretching his stiff arm in-between the threshold.

Who this niggah think he is? If this muthafucka knows like I do, he better get the fuck out my way. That's the problem with these cops, all that dirty ass pride they cling to after taking that lil short ass class thinking they run shit. By the end of this conversation he's going to know whose world he's in.

"Hey!" Sheriff Paul shouts out, "let Mr. Staxx through."

All the authority in the world can never replace confidence. When you're a wimp at heart your spirit knows when you aren't a match for competition. Status is earned! A niggah that took a six month class can't hold a candle to me! In my day you had to go out and demand your stripes or they'd be taken away from you. No one is going to hold your hand in this lifetime; they are either going to want to be in your shoes when you make it or laugh at you when you fall. There is no in-between. If you really sit down and pay attention your chest tells you the truth more than anything you see on TV Instead, we allow our children to be trained as puppets, confusing the fake with the real. Then they get taken out by the same muthafuckas that claim to serve and protect.

I eye the officer, "come on Tristian."

Paul is one of the OG Sheriffs of California State Prison who already knows how I get down. We go way back since my first day on the field representing as a defense attorney. Him, like every other officer in the building, knows my track record. I can win a case with my eyes closed in a hot tub on a Sunday morning.

Sheriff Paul walks us to the judge's chambers, "excuse Mr. Barkley, he's one of our new officers."

Twisting on my watch, "it's fine I know how these new cops can be," I reply, "I'm aware my assistant told you how important this client is?"

"Yes, Mr. Staxx," he pauses, "and with her not being present I'm assuming this young man is your new assistant."

I grin back at Tristian then Paul before answering his question. I had been caught on to Paul's sneaky links with that whore of an assistant of mine. Word around the office spreads faster than a wildfire. Everyone knows how she gets down; people just want easy. I get it, why turn down a quick fuck when your wife is irking your last nerve.

"Yes, I had to let her go."

"Oh, if you don't mind me asking what'd she do?"

"Let's just say the complaints about her unprofessional behavior outweighed her good work."

"Well, that's too bad to see someone with so much talent allow a bad attitude to get in the way of their success."

Him staring ahead in some sort of long daze makes the situation more weird than it has to be. We both know the real reason he's sad to see that fat ass go. We all loved that strong neck of hers, especially when the veins pop out the side. But let me stop reminiscing before me and this dude get into a silent beef.

"Uhm-uhm, so court is getting ready to start. I have to greet my client."

"Oh yes," shaking his head, "and hey," his voice lowers, "I want to thank you again for getting Jr. probation, the press was going to have a field day if shit got out there."

I tug on his shoulder, "yeah, don't mention it," smiling, "that is what I do."

Tristian and I head into the Judge's office. Like I said before there are no favors in the world, only trades. The apple doesn't fall far from the tree in his family, like his old man, Paul Jr. couldn't keep his hands to himself . Only difference is he jumped into the wrong young black woman's bed at the campus. So many young women spoke up that daddy's money could no longer keep the school board quiet, so he hired me to handle it. I thought it wouldn't be that bad to use his White privilege to my advantage. Why? Well, why not?

Now you know me already. There will never be a man who I fear on this earth, however being 100 percent aware of an enemy will always be my M.O. No weapon formed against my black ass is prospering. You have to know how to beat your opponent at their own game. However in this current case that dropped on my desk a few months ago it seems that a King forgot that falling is all part of the game. One thing about getting too far ahead of yourself is that you forget that you are too far ahead of yourself.

Chapter 4

Freedom Wanted

"Hello officer, please give my client and I a few moments to speak."

"Yes Sir."

I take one more look at Tristian trembling in the doorway. I understand his fear, the body language of this buff dude facing life but sitting cozy in the Judge's chair like he runs the world and shit.

Time to face the real music. And not none of that trash ass 69 soundtrack mess. I mean the Boosie Badazz shit before he went to the pen the first time...Javeon McCleaton. One of the most notorious gang banga's from the projects. Anyone can run with any set and carry their stripes, it's when that same muthafucka has sets like the Cholos', the British Mafia that make muthafuckas bow down. This niggah even has police force motorcycle gangs running for him.

"Aye bruh so what's this I hear about some for sure witness working with the prosecution?"

Aww man. Here we go with this shit. Every time he feels like he heard some info before me he forces me to remind him who calls the shots around this muthafucka.

I say, "I'm aware of this but it is indeed under control you don't have anything to worry about."

Scooting closer to the desk his wrists yank against the handcuffs.

"Niggah. You fucking lucky I let these crackas keep these shackles on."

The veins popping out of his forehead says it all, I'll have to cut into his ass to remind him wassup with me. I never been a lame nor a run over.

Looking over my shoulder at Tristain, "hey why don't you go wait out in the hallway and tell

Sheriff Paul we'll be ready in a few moments."

He stared back for a few seconds, "are you sure Sir?"

"Damn lil' niggah you can't hear?" Javeon snarks at Tristian, "you better get the fuck on before I help you get the fuck on... you dig?"

"Oh! Uhm-yes, yes Sir- I dug... I-I mean I dig," opening the door, "I'll see myself out." *Shutting the door.*

"Damn niggah!" I whisper loudly, "don't talk to my fucking assistant like that."

Jumping up from the desk, "what you gonna do pussy? "Huh?!" "you gone get that nice ass suit dirty?" He pauses again, "better yet, you gone show me the real you and throw away this plastic ass version you created for the press niggah."

If I lose my coo' I'll put this punk ass boy in the dirt myself. It's best to keep a level head especially since I have Tristian on my hip today. At the same time we both know what's really up with me. I don't have shit to prove to dude.

"You know what?" Taking a few steps back, "you are my client and I understand your frustration. I am well aware of the witness the prosecution thinks they have but I am also aware that even if this witness states you were at the warehouse your alibi is rock solid."

He takes a few breaths, "yeah, I'm aware of that," taking a seat, "but an insider told me that there are several witnesses."

"Well, since we have the advantage of the known, I am liable to get those witnesses dismissed before they're able to bring them out on the stand and..."

He cuts in. "bruh ain't no time for that ol' optimum shit."

"You been in prison for five years and aren't taking any classes, it's optimism my guy."

"Man. You know what the fuck I mean, I know one of the witnesses and this shit can fall back on you if you don't handle this shit accordingly so I'm not as worried as you should be."

This man will try anything to knock me off my square. There is no way humanly possible that my name can be tied up in the bullshit life he chose for himself. I ain't the type to judge, but on the other hand I did my time for all the sins I committed. This case goes down in history as my biggest mistake. It was some shit I was forced to handle or I would've never picked it up.

"Bullshit." My chest tightens, "I left the game long before you made a mess," easing to the desk,

"I don't have nothing to do with the way you threw your life away." *Knock. Knock.*

"We have to head out in a few here gentlemen." Officer Paul says.

Javeon goes on, "you remember that bum ass niggah you used to live off of? What was bruh name?"

Looking back at the door. "Coming out now Sheriff." I say, "Drew? I heard he died a few years back."

"Negative," he lifts up, "but one thing I'm positive about is if you don't take care of the situation, his snitch ass is going to blow yo' ass up on that stand too."

What the fuck just happened? This can't be happening right now. This muthafucka has to be out of his slow ass mind to tell me the that the same niggah that was going to be the best man at my wedding if I ever had one is a rat? Drew always been a lot of things but one thing he never proved to be was pussy. Besides him being low key sick, his loyalty to the hood never budged, especially for the brothers.

"Turns out he's been an informant hiding out in protective custody since I got locked up for this bullshit," he calls out, "guard, come on."

"So get one of your men on his head to keep him from taking a stand."

"Ahh, now there is the real 'Devine'," he grins with a straight face, "you think if I knew where this punk was hiding out we would be having this convo."

"So what's the problem?"

"We lost him, Ace. Now he's your problem so fix it." *The door opens.*

The guard says, "ready when you are boss."

He jumps up from behind the desk then heads out of the door.

Aww man! Maybe I was meant to pick up this case. One major issue I have is the fact that if I do find him, one way or another he has to go. The main thought replaying in my mind is, how does one man so tied to the streets become a snitch? What made this niggah bow to the system? We both made a pact that if one of us made it out we would put the other on to game. A few years after I left the state I heard through the grapevine he got hit by a car crossing the street. I guess that was the cover story for witness protection. I don't know how I got fooled. I guess I was so bent on living a new life I didn't care much about doing more research into his death. Or faked death in this case.

The streets never been for the weak. They viewed black men who had to go out to provide for their families as a failure. In addition to the system set up to prosecute our people in every way possible the streets just expanded the killing spree. The percentage of black men that are more likely to take out another brotha with a gun is astonishing. I lived through it all, the guns, the dope fiends, and pimps tricking hoes. Shit, I was one of those young niggahs not too long ago. You tend to look at the youth in the media and wonder what the hell is going on in their heads. Everyone is lost as fuck. You go from that moment in your childhood when you wished you were white because you binge watched hella white actors on the television who were living good ass lives meanwhile you in the jungle hoping you can get noodles for your next meal. Don't ever mistake my truth for 'ridicule' it's called holding the other race accountable for throwing stones and hiding their hands. We only fight for equality then get ridiculed. Be real, jealousy is the worst trait anyone can hold onto. It started a whole nation of agony for 400 years and counting.

"Hey Sir... Sir," Tristian enters the room, "the Sheriff says court is about to begin."

I tighten the knot on my tie, "yes... of course let's go."

Pacing myself on the elevator all the way into the courtroom has never been this hard. The more I figured out the secrets behind the system, the further I got in fucking the prosecutors up. Adding to why I can't stop thinking about how Drew violated; even him running around as one of Javeon's flunkies, turning evidence over to the courts leaves me all out of order. There's no telling what he'll say. Either way any known association to this man will ruin the empire I built from literal blood. He has to be stopped for sure.

Damn. Heading into the courtroom takes my thoughts back to the sexy ass moan Keisha has when she screams my name. She over there lookin' all fierce like one of them fine black Statues of Liberty and shit. Meanwhile her dickhead partner in crime on her side looking like he needs another bite of the Big Mac he left in the car.

"Mr. Staxx... Mr. Staxx." Judge Rowling's voice echoes in one ear out of the other, "does the defense have any statements against the prosecution's argument?"

"Yes, your Honor," clearing my throat, "seeing that there is no dangerous record of my client, and this is his first serious offense I think it is best that my client is granted bail."

Wrinkles pop out of Keisha's forehead, "your Honor, the Prosecution is very aware that Javeon

McCleaton's adult record is indeed squeaky clean...."

Judge Rowling cuts in, "then what is the hold up on Mr. McCleaton's bond?" Bingo. I got Judge Rowling tucked right inside the pocket of my suit.

"However," her teeth glows up the room, "Mr. McCleaton's juvenile records says otherwise."

"Your Honor, the defense pulling out childhood records is merely an attempt to lead the jury astray," I speak up, "my client has proven to be a law-abiding citizen who owns several McDonald Corporations, which makes sense to why his adult record is squeaky clean."

"I agree with Mr. Staxx," Judge Rowling says.

I smirk at Keisha.

"Although... Miss Turner does have a point about the childhood records," he says, "your client's file has quite a few complaints against him and even though he was never charged I'm troubled by the accusations against Mr. McCleaton."

I butt in, "and yes your Honor we are mindful of the offenses, but I am also aware that those charges were immediately dropped and confessed to be false allegations by the alleged victims."

"Or someone paid the victims off," Mr. Fat Face chimes in again.

"Objection your Honor!" I holler out.

"Sustained," Judge Rowling says, "Miss Turner, if you are going to have your second chair at your side I recommend you remind him that there are no disrespectful outbursts tolerated in my courtroom."

As much as I want to turn that frown painted on her face upside down with some of this good pipe I have to remind Big John to stay calm. She knows Bobby's ass has no filter anyways. He acts like the world owes him something. I always wondered what his problem was. It's no one else's fault he chose to sell his soul just to end up riding a coattail. That's the problem in society today, most people want to get it the easy way. Once they do the damage of getting what they want they OD on some kind of drug or poison themselves with big bottles of Pat-Ron, Hennessy or some shit all because they think they're ready to handle the pressure and can't. The kind of pressure that you have to prepare for when you get it out the mud. The trials, tribulations of it all to get you ready to take on this evil fucked up world.

When you start asking the Universe for a miracle it gives you way more than what you asked for. Some muthafuckas think slouching on your game and sucking ass will get you to the 'top'. Few that have their hands out last long in the spotlight. You either do it the 'hard' way, or you settle for being a slave succa kissing the masters' ass. In my opinion anything worth having is worth working for. That's the difference between me and all the other cocksuckas in this industry.

"Seeing that there may be some sort of prejudice against my client by the Prosecution I want to file for dismissal of the juvenile along with the public records and have them removed from the motion of discovery."

Judge Rowling's eyes scan mine, "not so fast Mr. Staxx, I understand that Mr. Jeffery here needs table manners, but that does not justify public records not being presented against your client," he says, "with that being said I may consider granting the Prosecution's argument to present the juvenile records to the jury at trial."

"Mcht!" Javeon sucks his teeth, "man what dis' mean?"

Crouching over, "sit back," I whisper, "I already have a copy of your juvenile records; they can't do much with it."

Bobby rushes a folder up to the judge's desk.

The court is quieter than snow falling out the sky. The judge flips through the papers back to back. I can't tell what he's thinking but from the strong side eye he's giving the Prosecution I know it's a great chance we have this part pretty much wrapped up.

"Uh-um, besides the Rape 1 Offense from the deceased victim. I don't see anything here but a few minor misdemeanor charges for fighting in high school," he says.

Yeah! That's what I thought. No victim, no case. Keisha knows better than that.

He goes on, "but I do also see here where Mr. McCleaton has back to back offenses of drug trafficking from the seventh grade all the way up to his tenth grade year in high school."

"Yes, your Honor, my client takes full accountability that he has made some mistakes in his childhood and is not conjuring up excuses; however, being without both your parents while taking care of multiple siblings in one household at the age of 15 holds a ton of responsibility."

The judge locks eyes with Javeon for a few seconds.

Come on man. Did Thing One and Two really think an ancient record would come between my client's case and my mouth piece. They've been trying to nail this dude's head to the wall for at least 10 years only managing to hem him up once. Still coming up with Jack shit, they had to know I'd eat their bullshit argument up for lunch. If he was my client when he first went in two years ago we both would have been on an island somewhere.

"Mr. Staxx I understand the circumstances of your client's childhood experiences and the court sympathizes with Mr. McCleaton's burden of caring for his siblings, but unlawful possession of Schedule III, IV or V controlled substances is a felony and punishable by a 1 to 5-year term of incarceration," turning the page, "which looks like at age 16 your client served a 2 year sentence at Ross in the state of Ohio."

I speak up, "Your Honor, I had many clients from the state of Ohio before and it seems that there aren't strict laws for citizens who are detained for marijuana trafficking."

Keisha cuts in. "Your Honor with this amount of proof from the defendants' records the State would like to add that the defendant is indeed a major flight risk. And our key witness can surely attest to that."

Damn, she can't wait to bury a niggah under the jail cell. Trying to barge her way into the door ain't gone help in this situation. I know what kind of game she tryna play. She thought giving up a dead end witness would throw me off so she could hand me my ass in court. *Nah.* It's going to take more than a tight pussy to knock me off my game. Pretty soon she is going to realize I invented the game. If I can beat a white man at his own game she is going to have to come way harder than this.

"Your Honor," clearing my throat, "if you allow me to present the evidence that my client is innocent of the drug charges in his childhood I think the court should reconsider granting bail for my client."

The judge peeps over at Keisha then back to me.

"Bailiff," he says.

Handing off the files that Tristian hands over I take a soft breath. The first thing that came to mind is how shitty Keisha is about to be when I blow up her little attempt to wrap the jury around her finger. Except I only see her hands being wrapped around something else, if you know what I mean.

Putting forth my fingers tapping on the desk, "if you turn to page 3, paragraph one it states that Officer Barkley, the officer who arrested my client took a leave of absence 1 year after my client went to jail."

"Well, I can say the laws in Ohio are quite different and I do see here that the Officer was indeed let go for his unfit practices of the law but what does this have to do with your client and his track record of drug trafficking Mr. Staxx?"

I go on, "and if you turn to page 5 the first paragraph in the summary defines my client's aunt who was sole guardian at the time. She along with 30 other citizens filed over 100 complaints on this officer, who seemingly found 1 pound of marijuana on a 15 year old walking home from school. Indeed it was later discovered that my client had less than 100 grams in his pocket which in the state of Ohio carries a fine of one-hundred and fifty dollars."

Flipping the page, "mhm, I see," his eyes glued on the paper, "and I also see here where it states that your client's aunt filed a lawsuit against the Lucas county jail for Officer Barkley's misconduct."

"Smiling at Keisha, "and you can also see that my client's aunt left this earth, leaving the lawsuit up in flames, but my client only served a two out of a five year sentence in the juvenile detention center for presenting good behavior," shifting my head towards the Judge, "after this he never sees another charge nor a day in the court again."

Like I said once before, I am the definition of the G.O.A.T. I understand that saying never is not supposed to be in a black man's vocabulary but the kind of self-assurance I walk around this bitch with can make a nun swear. Looks like Keisha's pet didn't do as much research as she thought his ass did. Even if he did, there is no way both of them combined had access to the same resources I do. I have connects in every state you can think of. Them hoes could NEVER!

Rule number five; it's not about what you know, it's who you know.

Bobby's lips mutter, "your Honor the prosecution is sympathetic for Mr. McCleaton's childhood however we do not find it acceptable to go around taking people out and dealing drugs because mommy made a few mistakes."

I speak out. "Objection your Honor."

"Sustained," Judge's eyebrows raise up, "Miss Turner, this is your last warning, get your assistant in line or get out of my courtroom!"

"Your Honor I do apologize for Mr. Jeffery's outburst," squeezing Bobby's shoulder, "nonetheless he does hold some truth in his vile statement." She says, "minus the childhood records the state of California has been building a case on Mr. McCleaton for over ten years and within those years we have gathered plenty of evidence on the defendant, street name Spider, who was caught red handed in the warehouse on November 29, 2019, in a shootout with law enforcement, leaving three officers deceased and one comatose."

"Yes," Judge Rowling adds in, "I see here that the defendant was arrested on the scene but..."

"But" I jump in, "my client's fingerprints weren't discovered on any of the weapons in the warehouse. Nor has forensics found any fingerprints from my client on any of the bullets from the deceased nor the comatose officer's bodies."

There is no possible way Javeon is walking out of here with those handcuffs on his wrist. I dazed into the air for a minute imagining the bright sun shining on my face once this case is out of my hands for good. Getting my life back on track is the most important gift I can think of right now. I just hope Keisha can forgive me for ruining her reputation for getting muthafuckas disbarred. This is the last year this case is making it to. 2019, my year to win the biggest case against the baddest prosecution team in California. Of course the second best office if you compare my legal team of sharks I recruited throughout the years.

"Mhm," the Judge mumbles, "interesting. I see that."

Without hesitation, "in spite of what the FBI or forensics presented," Keisha says, "Mr. McCleaton was still apprehended in the act of what we believe was a cash exchange between defendant Jabril Dupree, street name, Thrash, who is a known drug distributor."

"Your Honor..."

"Stop," Judge Rowling cut me short, "I have heard enough, now, I understand the passion of both of you, however, save the good arguments for the jury." Taking a breath, "I see that your client does not have any criminal trail denouncing his involvement up to this point so... I am going to throw out both the public and juvenile records."

"Thank you, your Honor." I jump in.

I knew it! Only a matter of minutes before he's being processed out of the system, and I get to do whatever the fuck I please with my life. May even take Tristian to celebrate with some loose pussy at that strip joint over there on twentieth and main.

I can peep the slight tears almost crowding Keisha's vision. Momma taught me to never make a woman cry but the kind of joy this victory's about to bring I can't bring myself to put her emotions over it.

"However, with the Prosecution's motion of discovery the court does find Mr. McCleaton a flight risk and denies the grant for bail."

His gavel thumps down.

Chapter 5

That Other Word For Responsible

"What!" Javeon whispers loudly.

I pat down on his shoulder, "relax."

"Fuck that! You said you was gone get me up out this muthafucka today niggah." Bawling his lips up, "don't forget our agreement."

I mumble, "you have to remain calm so these muthafuckas will look at you like a product of your environment and not a menace to society."

Fuck! Fuck! Fuck! A million damn sirens went off in my head. If I didn't know any better I would say I was so wrapped up in my pride that I didn't see this coming. I learned a long time ago it doesn't matter who you have stuffed into your pocket if you don't have your eyesight clear in the game of longevity you'll lose every time.

Bobby nods, "thank you, your Honor."

"Don't thank me yet." Judge Rowling comments, "this case has been going on for quite some time and the court is ready to move on," looking at Keisha, "so Miss Turner I advise you to have all your I's dotted and T's crossed."

"Yes your Honor," she responds, "we will be ready."

"Court is adjourned."

Javeon turns to me, "man you better fix this! And I mean that shit."

I return a quick head bob as the Bailiff takes him back to the cells.

With the amount of expectation Javeon wants from me I have to damn near bleed to win this case. We have a short lived victory today, and I believe the small wins will equal a larger reward. On the other hand dudes like Javeon living a fast life don't appreciate the art of waiting. It's either his way or the ditch on the side of the highway.

Tristian packs up all the files and puts them in my suitcase.

"That was really intense Boss."

I get a glimpse of the small smirk extending Keisha's lips. *Oh.* Most men see her confidence as a threat to their egos. Me? I think that shit sexy as hell. That's one of the things I like about her. I love a woman who can stand her ground. Not letting her guard down too easy.

"Yeah," staring at Keisha, "go wait at the elevator, I'll meet you there."

I pace myself going towards her in enough time for Bobby to pack his suitcase up and go in the other direction.

Squeezing in-between her and the stand "you think you're big time don't you?" I ask.

She looks me up and down.

"Mhm," she comments, "don't you have anything better to do than trying to bribe the Prosecution?"

"Oh baby girl there's no need for payoff," closing in on her, "I just want to make sure that there isn't going to be any bad blood between us when my client walks free."

One thing I know for sure is how beneficial it is to get into your opponent's head. Besides, we both are familiar with having a good time outside of work while fucking shit up in the courtroom.

"Oh baby boy, we both know who's laughing last. And it'll be me, laughing at your client's face the second he has to keep those chains on his wrist."

Grabbing her suitcase off of the table she heads out of the double doors.

Damn this woman plays good as hell. *Whew!* She most definitely has all the potential it takes to make a niggah chase after her fine ass. I may have the upper hand with info, still if she finds out that I do, she'll send that corny bald dude out to ruin everything.

Time for Plan B... If anyone's going to find my old pal, Drew, my boy Lethal is. It's been damn near a decade since I last saw him. Making it out the hood made it easy to disappear. Once you get to a big city your home town is basically dirt, turning the people you used to run with a non-factor. In my case running with a crowd of low-lifers clicked in my head every time I thought about going back. Even if I laid low I had nothing to go back to. All my folks were either dead or locked up.

One year muthafuckas got capped so much that death became immune. It was just another dumb brutha taking out his homeboy, sister, or even his main mans. What's it to live for when the one thing you wake up for is catching the next body to up your street cred. I started to see niggahs as weak links the third time Jehovah gave me a chance at life. Fatalities can get addicting, not only the gun sounds but the vibration you feel when that bullet leaves the chamber. The stamina that sparks a light up in your soul, it's like your body leaves the ground with all the power you have in your hands. Believe me, I know.

Tristian walks through the doors.

"Boss, the driver gave me a buzz, he is waiting out front."

I nod, "yes let's get out of here."

As we're on the elevator I watch the numbers count down each floor we pass.

"So," Tristian clears his throat, "I just want to say that was the most intense bond hearing I've ever witnessed."

"Mhm," turning my watch over, "wasn't it?"

My foot drags across the floor waiting for the elevator to hit the ground floor. I can't stop thinking about the shit show I've gotten myself into. Javeon, Keisha, her pet hippo Bobby who can never shut the fuck up. And that look, the way Keisha mugs him every time he opens his big ass mouth. By far she is one of the greatest lawyers in the state, top of her class. But has a gremlin as her assistant on a case this big. Something isn't right.

"Tristian, you handled yourself well in there," turning to him, "I'd like to make you my new assistant."

His mouth drops, "wow! Really!"

"Really," I say, "now come on we have work to do."

"Yes Sir."

To think this year was going to be an easy year. In the grinding period of yo' life you think once you make it to the top that all your problems fade away. All those late nights, early mornings you pray and wish that you can taste a mil, and swear you gone do right by it. You picture yourself in the sand poppin' bottles and shit, right? Wrong. When you make it to the top you have to stay active in order to stay at the top. Unless you sitting on billions of dollars which should be the real dope boy dream. Instead, we run in circles.

"Mr. Staxx," the driver holds on the car door, "time to grab you a new phone."

He pulls off into traffic.

Sliding through the contacts in my phone I scroll to the very last unsaved number in my phone. A part of me don't know if I hate more the fact I have to hit this dude up or that I held onto his number. Knowing Lethal, his old school ass has the same number from ten years ago. Lord knows I made a promise to myself that the day I send him a text of any kind, I hit rock bottom. Or I really have a mess on my hands that needs the kind of cleaning I can't be a part of by any means. This is a decision I can never turn back from. Question is, am I willing to summon the grim reaper from the dead?

"So Tristian, now that we're upping your pay grade I have your first assignment."

"Yes Sir, I took a few notes through the years... your cup of coffee in the morning, black two sugars, three creamers, set all of your meetings the day before and make sure to remind you to take at least one break a day."

"Woah," cutting him off, "slow down a second... wait, you've been paying that much attention."

This dude is way more committed than I give him credit for. He remembers more than Alesha dirty ass ever did. I should have got rid of her rat ass a long time ago. I can already tell he's going to be the best person to have on my side to get through this case.

"Well, I thought... I-I always hoped that the day came where I would be your assistant. I always said to myself that one day I would be able to learn as much as I can from you," he smiles, "even seeing you today, the way you owned Miss Keisha Turner like it was nothing speaks volumes Sir."

My soft smirk fades aways, "actually that's what your new assignment is going to consist of. As you can see Miss Turner is very experienced..."

"Yes, she actually passed her California bar exam with a score of 279 which is way past average considering the 34 percent pass rate in the state."

My eyes shoot out at him.

"I'm sorry Sir!" He bursts out, "too much?!" I get quiet for a few seconds.

Then I say, "no kid, you're doing great, I actually need you to do some deep research on Miss Keisha for me."

"Of course, what kind of research are we talking?"

Before I hired Tristian I looked into his background. I found some interesting facts on the Ivy-league graduate of Yale. Let's just say his father's divorce money helped cover his ass from getting put out of school for almost overdosing in his buddy's dorm room. Meaning keeping his mouth shut about a little off the grid digging shouldn't be a problem.

"I'm not the one to keep tabs on people's lives, however having information is powerful." I say.

I can see the spit drying up in his mouth.

"Uh-uhm, wha-what, may I ask what you are referring to?"

Looking him dead in his soul, "let us just say I am aware of your expunged records that allowed you to walk across that Yale stage," leaning in, "your mother loves her son very much."

He looks down at the seat.

"But that is neither here nor there, we all make mistakes," I say, "now, I need you to do a thorough search on Keisha. I mean bank statements, family members, if you find out how many times she takes a shit I want to know."

We sit in silence.

"Of course Sir," he asks, "one thing though."

"And what's that?"

"Miss Turner has been in the field for over ten years. I don't have that kind of access to..."

Cutting him short, "don't worry about it, my people will contact you. All you have to do is answer the phone."

Here goes nothing. A kid like Tristian didn't have the balls to fuck up my trust. You have to not only know how to play the game you have to also stand on yo' shit. No matter the obstacle at hand, only thing that matters is you coming out on top.

"We have arrived Sir," my driver looks back at us.

I say to Tristian. "Walk with me."

Just at the moment we get out of the car I send a text to the unsaved number in my phone. *3151 Citrus St. Lemon Grove, CA 91945-2214... Ace.*

"So now that you are in with the big dogs we're going to grab new phones."

We head into the store.

"Oh okay Sir," he asks, "may I ask the reason we need new phones?"

Searching around for the best iPhone they carry in this joint is my main goal. The point of having the best shit wherever you go is to stop people from asking questions they don't need to ask. Although you see the richest white folks walking around in the oldest new balance's in stock, most of them don't get racially profiled. But when you see a black man in the store dressed up in a white tee and black forces, the first thought is that he's about to steal something. That goes for anything.

Don't mistake my skill for 'the broke boy mindset', we gonna focus on the reverse psychology of it all. I'm not saying go out and spend all yo' money trying to look good when you broke as fuck.

I'm saying, when you get to a point in yo' life where you ballin' out like a niggah like me you have to it only play the part but look it. We still get seen as that corner boy in the 'wrong' neighborhood, that's why you gotta know how to talk that shit.

"Oh, I like this one Sir," he points at an iPhone 10, "I would like this one."

Grabbing it out his hand, "okay, take it up to the counter, I'll be up there in a second."

I keep looking for the phone I want, it's been years since I had to replace my phone, but I don't want to take any chances. Plus, in a nice ass Xfinity store like this one having so many iPhones to choose from. I come across an all gold iPhone XR. *Ouu!* This me right here. I think to myself, flipping it to the back, this thang got three cameras too. I talk about keeping style, but I feel old ass fuck still carrying around the iPhone 7. I just never had a reason to have one camera let alone two. Let me check up out of here before I end up spending more than a thousand dollars than I need too.

"Excuse me Sir can I help you with something," a small voice peaks out of the corner.

I peep Tristian standing at the counter before I decide if I'm going to politely put this broad in her place for questioning a king.

"No, but I think you can..."

As soon as I look up my mouth almost falls to the floor. *Man what!* I can't believe my eyes right now.

"Radiance!" Both my eyes light up.

"Devine Staxx," she smirks, "how have you been?!"

My heart damn near stops beating in my chest the second our eyes lock. Radiance Marie. I haven't seen this woman in years. The first thing that comes to mind is *keep your cool bro.*

She grabs my neck up inside of her arms, "it's so nice to see you again Devine," her fruity breath brushes against my ear, "you look great."

The way we're standing here embracing each other's bodies feels like we left the ground.

Backing up, "uh-uhm, so it's been a while huh?" I ask.

"Yes, she smiles, six years?"

Scratching my ear, "seven," I correct her.

Both of our eyes cling on to each other. I don't have the slightest idea of what is going through this woman's head. All I can think about is the way her grown woman body formed into one sexy ass dark chocolate Coca-Cola bottle. And I'd happily drink every ounce of that muthafucka up in the middle of the aisle right now.

"Everything okay boss," Tristian cuts in.

Oh, yes!" Rubbing my neck, "yes this is an old friend.

"Boss." She says.

"Tristian this is Radiance, Radiance this is my assistant, Tristian."

"Nice to meet you ma'am," he says.

If I don't end this conversation now there ain't no telling what the next words will be coming out of my mouth.

I say, "so we have to head out to handle some business."

The soft twist in her lips says it all. Even after all these years she still wants me, not like one of those quickies like back in the day. She wants more than that long stroke I used to fuck her world up with. Her spirit craves long walks on the beach, midnight drives on the highway on the way into the city, intense deep strokes that shifts her soul into a different reality. One she'd never imagined herself reaching before. Or that could just be what I want.

"Oh sure!" reaching down into her purse, "well here is my card, "biting on her lip, "you can call me anytime."

I look down at the card. *Rose Gold Sculpting.* It says.

"Sure," I say, "see you around."

Her fine ass walks out of the door, leaving my balls dropping on the floor. *This woman here boy!* She already knows how to get a niggah all tongue tied and shit. On top of her being all natural makes me wanna grab her ass up to take her back to my house.

Then my logical voice kicks in, *Get yo' head out of the gutta bro.* If anything, linking back up is the worst mistake to make. The last time I saw her was the last kiss we've ever exchanged. I remember feeling like the world finally came crashing down on my shoulders.

"Yes baby! Almost there! Uhh! Uhh!"

The neighbors could hear Radiance screaming my name up and down the street. My head was so far up that tight ass dress she had on I couldn't even wheeze for air if I wanted too.

I grumbled back, "you like that baby?"

We sat on the edge of Mount Lee for hours. Talking, laughing, making love, it all made a niggah heart sink in his chest and shit. Radiance was always the kind of woman who listened to your problems without a speck of judgment. She made it clear that when she loved she would love you until the end of time. And I loved her right back.

"Wait, wait, wait, wait," she pulled on my ears, "we still haven't talked about the move."

Here she go again with this shit. No matter how many times I shared with her my concerns about her wanting to suddenly leave the city it interrupted our 'bedtime'. So I decided to keep my mouth shut about it. That never stopped her from bringing it up though.

She sits up, "baby I'm serious, I know you're working on getting your degree, but they have great schools in Ohio too."

I twist the cracks out of my neck before I reply.

"Radiance," easing closer to her, "I know you said you have to be by your sister's side," I said, "but I don't see the reason why you'd have to drop everything and go."

Her back dropped back down to the sheet we laid out on the grass.

With the blank mug roughing up her cheekbones and shit I knew she was about to let me have it but to my surprise she didn't. There was plenty of times when Radiance made it her mission to let me know what she didn't like. What she wasn't going to put up with, and that was the main reason why I fucked with her the way I did.

"So you're not going to say anything?" I asked.

"Nope," she replied, "you made your mind up and I can't make you do anything."

"So what? That's it? "You're just going to up and leave because of your sister? What about the sculpting business you were going to start back home in L.A?"

"What I tried to tell you yesterday is they have a few buildings in Cleveland for leasing that I'm going to be able to afford in a few months."

My Adam's apple thumped harder than the beat in my fucking chest. I felt more than a lame to let myself have feelings for anybody, especially after Trisha left my life.

"Look Devine, I love you," rubbing her hand across my face, "but my sister needs me back in Ohio and I know you don't want to back track to your hometown for whatever reason, but I can't stay here either."

"It's not that I don't want to backtrack... it's just that I don't..."

Chapter 6

Recognizing Havoc

I *look up at the lights on the Hollywood sign. My mind was racing with so many thoughts that I had to take to the grave with me that I just wanted the conversation to be over with. There was no need to bring up my past to explain why I didn't want to take that next step with the woman I loved to death.*

Seeing the last few tears dropping down both sides of her face as she walked down the hill tore my insides the fuck up. I made sure to never allow myself to deal with another woman the same way I did with Radiance.

A few months after she left I started to go in on my school work. For a minute I thought if I worked harder my mind would forget all about her. But after hitting my first 'M', every once in a while I thought about seeing the look on her face when she walked through the front door of my big house. Only thing about time is that it waits for no one. I, for one, drilled that inside of my head a long time ago, that love shit is for the birds.

"Will this be all, Sir?"

The lil dude at the front counter slides our phones across the scanner.

"Yes," I say.

"That will be two thousand even Sir."

My mind is completely blown. Who would have thought in a million years this woman walks in my life. Leaving me to thirst for her touch. She still smells the same, talks the same with that little twitch in her lip when she's lowkey happy as hell. For so long I wanted her to at least see how I live. The other half didn't want anything to do with her or the split in my chest after she left.

We head out of the store.

"She seems pretty nice," Tristian says.

Ignoring him on the way to the car I look both ways before we cross the street.

There is one thing I know for a fact that I can't allow her presence to get in the way of what I got going on. There is enough dramatic shit in my circle right now, adding some miracle pussy in the equation is not going to make it better. You see with a woman like Radiance who always stands her ground, suck good, alongside loving the shit out of you is a dangerous combination.

"Back to the office Mr. Staxx?" The driver asks.

Getting in the car, "we are both going home," I say, "and step on it."

"Will do."

Shutting the door behind us, he gets in then takes off into the main road.

"I want to thank you for the new phone Sir," Tristian says.

Staring out of the window I nod in response.

"Toss your old phone then send me your new number and let Terry know that you are my new assistant in the morning."

"Okay Sir, is he going to fill in for me?"

"Yes," I say, "let Linda know to set up interviews starting with the list on applications on Indeed."

"Noted."

He sends me his number then I send a text to my associates with his number attached. *Deep BG check into Keisha Turner call 323-874-0986 with the information.*

By the time we drop Tristian off at his house and pull up to mine my mind is fried. Thousands of thoughts crashing in my skull has my head hurting like hell. *Man.* My life wasn't this fucked a few months ago. All I can think about is how I'm going to push Keisha's big ass in a corner to shut her defense down against my client. With Tristian on my case I have a higher chance at spoiling her little plan of destroying my office's name to make hers look better.

My driver waves me off as I walk up to my door.

Home sweet fucking home. With the kind of day I had I wouldn't mind taking a day off to soak tomorrow. Knowing me though I ain't gone ever have time to take a day off. I made a promise to myself that when I open my second office in Georgia I will take more days to myself. I'm not going to lie either, a part of me is scared as hell to be without work. I wouldn't know what to do. I mean I can get on a boat, cruise the city or something like that. Yeah, money comes in regardless of me showing up, I just feel more comfortable when I'm physically racking in my bread.

My back hit the bed as my shoes hit the floor. Sometimes I wish to have a fine ass woman lying under the cover butt naked with my plate already in the microwave. I picture Radiance's soft ass lips caressing mine over and over. The way she looked today is on replay in my head. She lowkey knows she can have this muthafucka anytime she wants too. My lips damn near stretch from ear to ear while I sink into the pillow.

After all the drama I made it back to my nice ass house, spreading out on a big ass king size bed, and most important is the peace I always feel at home. No one can take this kind of relief away from a niggah.

I admire the gold blades spinning on my ceiling fan until I doze off.

Lethal's scratchy ass voice shouts out.

"Aye bro come on you know I come with all the heat!"

"Yeah right niggah, I'm gone tear yo ass up with these lucky hands." I laugh.

We're sitting in the middle of 19th street outside of granny's house. I used to love Tuesday nights because the dopeheads wanted more dope and I got to bust the homies head in the dice game.

"Ouu! Ustedes niggahs no pueden tocar me!" Lethal said.

"Man what I tell you about speaking that no comprende Espanol shit man." Drop looked at Lethal.

Although I lived in the house with Drop I never liked his hating ass. He was one of them niggahs that always had something to say because he never got no pussy. For real, for real, I used to think bruh was on the downlow. I mean, I wouldn't of gave a fuck what he did in his life. But that also didn't give him the right to act like a lame all the time.

Lethal kept his eyes focused on the dice game, "I'll do you a favor and disregard your disrespect," he said, "because you don't know who I am."

Drop took after one of those dudes that had to have the last laugh. After almost dropping his ass a few times I found it best to mind the business that paid me when it came to him. And that muthafucka couldn't put a dime in my pocket.

"Mhm," Drop stood up, "Ace I suggest you get yo' boy before I send his ass, cold body, back to Mexico in one of them nice ass suits."

Damn. These fools always worried about the wrong type of shit. Why you so upset at how another man talked in a dice game? We all ran our mouths but every time I brought Lethal to make some extra money Drop had to run his fat ass mouth.

"Aye bro just leave that shit alone," I say to Lethal, "we don't need any trouble with this play on the line."

I met Lethal in the halfway house a few months after I got out the pen. He was of those quiet Mexicans who liked to duck off in the background. That's what I thought up until I witnessed him knock a man out in the blink of an eye. I knew I had to put him on game as soon as he hit the streets. His ethnicity may have been Black-Hispanic but that muthafucka had some of those tai-chi moves straight out of China. Some even referred to them as being Lethal.

Drop joins in, "yeah you betta listen to yo' master," he laughed, "with his proper talking ass."

"Con un solo golpe saldrás como una luz. Pussy." Lethal raised up."

Drop pushed up on Lethal, "Man I don't give a fuck about nothing you just said," grabbing on his waist, "but what I do know is I got something hot for you burning right inside my pocket."

Both of them hovered over me while I scoped out the other two homies on Drop's right. Them two bozos wasn't on shit. They was corny just like Drop.

I jumped up, "look! Both of y'all niggahs need to chill the fuck out before we do some shit you don't want to do." I said.

I kept my eyes focused on the other two niggahs standing behind Drop. We all lived under the same roof but that didn't mean nothing. Those boys hated the fact that Drew and I rocked harder without knowing each other as long as they did. The difference between me and them was I never made it my mission to kiss the next man's ass. Not even to get on. Drew respected that shit and gave me my space to do whatever the fuck I pleased.

I stand on the side of Lethal trying to get him to take a step back.

"I'll tell ya' what," Drop smiled, "since yo' mama likes black pipe tell her I got some BBC over here waiting on... aht!"

"Oh shit!" I shouted out.

In the blink of an eye blood splattered all through the air while Lethal's blade slid across Drop's neck. He left that man on his knees gasping out for air coddling his throat.

My first thought was to spare the homies but the second I saw them niggahs clutching on their heat survival mode kicked right in.

Pop! Pop! I dropped both of them boys like a light switch.

"Fuck!" I yelled out.

Pop! I sent another shot straight through Drop's head.

"Ace of Spades niggah!" I spat on Drop's body.

Lethal's hand gripped the back of my hoodie. That wasn't my first time having to blow a niggah brains back for talking too fucking much. It was the very first time in my life that I felt sorry for having to do so. I didn't feel an ounce of pity for Drop, it was not one but two of Drew's best hittas I had to take out.

Lethal and I laid low in an abandoned apartment until sun up.

"Hermano, we have to take that shit to the grave." He went on, "if your buddy Drew finds out you took out his brother we are going to be at war with half of Toledo."

I had no words to say. Picturing blood and brains all over the concrete. Three lifeless bodies drowning in thick puddles of blood. The only thing I could think of was the kind of person I became. A ruthless thug who didn't care about anyone or anything. A menace to society with no way out of war.

My eyes shoot right open to a cold piece of metal pinching my throat.

"Now wait a minute baby," the air in my lungs cringe, "we can talk this out."

I throw both my hands in the air the second the blur in my eyes clear up to see Alesha standing over my bed holding a big ass butcher knife to my neck.

What in the entire fuck is wrong with this bitch! I have never met someone this fucking crazy in my life.

She whispers in my ear, "what's the matter Jonathan? Don't have a strap on you?" She laughs.

"I have no idea who that is," I reply, "but I do know if you leave right now...I will forget that you ever broke into my house."

Despite the darkness I can feel every emotion she is feeling. I'm no stranger to a scorned woman and with these sharp ass blades prickling up against my throat it is clear she is more than pissed. I can tell I hit a harsh trigger inside her soul.

Trying to stop the spit from clogging up my airwaves I blow out a steep breath.

"Look baby, I know I hurt you... but we can talk about it without the knife."

Her body sits steady on top of mine. She isn't having none of the bullshit that's coming out of my mouth. On top of her seeming like she know too much about me. One way or another one of us ain't making it out of this muthafucka, and to be honest it's not going to be me. After all the shit I went through I bet all my money that I'll never be taken out by a bitch. I don't give a fuck how crazy she playing.

"You think you can just fuck me, make me promises like you love me and then fire me? Nah, you gone have to..."

I cut in, "look baby I'm sorry we can..."

"Shut up niggah!" She yells, "I know who you really are... Jonathan Greyhound," she pauses, "and I know you bought your firm with drug money. I know about the trail of bodies you left back in your hometown. All the licks you hit on the kingpins in your city, shit, you're one of the biggest gotdamn menaces in history."

Not a single thought is going through my head. All I know is she has my undivided attention. Inside, my body is so fucking hot that wood can burn on it.

"Look," lowering my voice to a whisper, "I don't know who you've been conversing with, but I have no idea who that..."

"Shut the fuck up!" Her grip on the knife tightens, "tell the truth! Your mother named you Jonathan Greyhound and after you got out of jail for the third time you changed your name and fled the state!"

Aww man! I don't have a clue how she found all this information out. But I will definitely find out, one way or another or whoever she talking to is going to have hell to pay.

"Aight," I say, "you got me. I grew up in the muthafuckin' trenches, slaying niggahs for less than a dime and breaking bitches down. I went from working my granny's prescriptions to being one of the coldest drug dealers in the state of Ohio by age 20."

We sit without a sound.

"Mhm, now that wasn't so bad," she mumbles, "so this is what's going to happen. You're going to continue to fuck me."

I suck in the air, "and then what?"

Her lips brush across my ear as her titties run across my chest.

"You're going to give me my job back," kissing on my neck, "and your little secret will be safe with me."

This bitch is more psycho than I thought. It's damn sure no secret that she had no kind of guidance growing up. But for her to think for a second that shit is about to go back to normal after she's obviously connected with someone deeply involved in my past life. Question is who? Who has she been in contact with that knew who I was, where I am now and who I became? I prayed so long, did plenty of work to invent a new, improved man. A better man who could wake up every morning not wishing someone would take him out of his misery. That can walk down the street without looking over his shoulder.

I go along, "okay," I huff, "pull that shit out," I say.

She pulls back the knife while our tongues cuddle on top of each other's back to back.

Putting it on my nightstand she pulls out my dick then slides it inside of her pussy head first.

"Ouu, that's right bitch have yo' way with this big ass dick."

I can feel the warm tears dripping from the side of her cheeks hitting my chest.

"Uhh!" Her voice shivers, "I-I love you."

Her warm walls get tighter and tighter around my dick, water gushing from inside her soaking up both my thighs.

"Look," gripping her face, "we can forget all about what went on tonight," I peck her lips, "but it's only under one condition."

She continues jumping up and down with her head facing the ceiling.

"And what's that, huh?" She moans, "what you need me to do daddy?"

For a second all this wet ass pussy dripping on my sheets distracted me from the real issue at hand. She has to find herself on the next bus ride out of the state if she wants to keep breathing. I'll do anything to keep my name safe and little Miss Know It All is about to find that out right now.

Sliding my hands up her back, "mhm," grumbling in her ear, "you have to leave the city... I'll provide you with all the cash you'll need for you and your son."

The way she stops in mid-air lets me know I got her fucked up. Unfortunately for her I don't give one fuck about how she feels. All I know is that she better take this deal before I get more mad than I already am.

"But... you said," she pauses, "you don't want me?"

"I do." I reply, "But with the amount of information you have about me can stir up a whole bunch of unwanted attention in my career baby... by the way where did you get this information from anyway?"

Again we sit in total silence, this time it feels like we both stopped breathing. In fact she was trying to figure out my next move, but I already know hers. Alesha's like a garden snake, okay to be around until they are in the wrong hands.

"I'll tell you what," she says, "I'll just let everyone know what you did to your little girlfriend."

"What?!"

"Yeah, Trisha right? I know all about..."

"Ahh!"

Without warning my fist smashes right into her skull. Knocking her off the bed I jump up and grab her up by the neck.

I bang her head up against the wall, "listen you little thot I tried to play nice with yo' ass but you really testing my fucking patience."

"Stop!" She wheezes out for air, "please stop I'm sorry! I'm sorry!"

Flashes of the last look I see on Trisha's face begging out for help sends red lights flashing into my eyes.

"It is indeed no secret that this young man hasn't had an easy life," Robert says, *"but that in no reason gives Mr. Greyhound the right to attempt to take justice into his own hands."* walking past the jury, *"which in closing sadly led him into taking out his own girlfriend, leaving her family,"* pointing to Trisha's mother, *"devastated. Thank you."*

Mr. Robert heads back to his desk.

"My client Mr. Greyhound has indeed been a victim in the harsh world of poverty."

My lawyer, Terry Tone, faced the jury while I twisted a water bottle I had since trial began that morning.

This was one of the worst days in my life. I hated myself for all the pain Trisha's momma felt alone.

My lawyer went on with his plea, "you see, there is no guidance in the neighborhood that my client comes from known as 'the ghetto' yet he still makes a way in his life to nurture the children," he said, "the Prosecution has no case strong enough here to hold my client on, only a witness statement from a well-known gang member who has made a deal of his own with the Prosec..."

"I object your Honor!" Mr. Robert cut in.

"Overruled," Judge Pettersen said, "Mr. Tone."

"Allow me to rephrase your Honor," just think about it," pacing in front of the jury, "my client is a well-known family man who takes care of his youngest brother as well as three other family members at his grandmother's home," blowing out a breath, "I'm just saying when you think about snatching another young black man's life away from 'hearsay', just ask yourself one thing before you go to bed at night... how was I a part of taking away a bright, young man's future?"

After the closing arguments we waited for the jury's conviction. My granny showed that she cared about me by getting the coldest lawyer in the city. Still I wanted to go to prison. I've never been, but to live my life on the streets without Trisha by my side was unimaginable. I didn't give one fuck about what happened to me after that night.

Judge Pettersen spoke up, "has the jury reached a verdict?" He asked.

One of the jurors stands, "yes your Honor," she answers.

"On the count of gang affiliation how do you find?"

"We find the defendant guilty, your Honor."

The moment they began to call out the verdicts my mind sat still. I had no words, no emotions, no anger, only pity. Not for myself at all, but for her family.

Judge Pettersen went on, "in the murder of first degree, how do you find?"

All the serving I did in the world couldn't add up to the amount of pain I felt from catching my first body. Let alone, it being the love of my life, I hated life itself. Accident or not, I didn't care what happened to me.

"With the lack of evidence provided by the prosecution we find the defendant not guilty, your Honor."

The courtroom could of went up in flames.

"Ahh! What?!" Trisha's mother yelled out. "I hate you! I hope you die!"

Words can't explain the agony eating my soul alive!

"I hate you!" I scream out. "I hate you!"

Veins buldge out of Alesha's forehead as soon as I drop her body to the ground.

"Ahh!" I yell out, "look what you made me do!"

I curl up into a big ass ball in the middle of my bedroom floor. *Fuck! Fuck! Fuck!* I can't even look her way. All I can do is cradle both my ears trying to block out the harsh wheezes coming from her mouth. This can't be happening to me! Why couldn't she just leave me the fuck alone. It feels like every time I take three steps forward I go six steps back.

"No, no, no," I cry to myself, "Lord take me! I can't do this shit no more."

Chapter 7

Say What You Mean
And Mean What You Say

A few more minutes and the voices inside my head gone make me take Alesha, then myself out. This shit is a never ending whirlwind of bullshit. Why am I here? To kill? To get killers out of jail for paper? Or to be a puppet to the slave master who runs this earth realm? None of this shit makes sense to me! I worked so hard to not only live a new life but invent a new fucking person to still be fucked over? *Nah.* This shit ain't right to me at all.

I'm about to end it all... not having enough willpower to rise up from the ground. I reach over her to slide to my nightstand drawer back then lay hands on my nine.

"You ready to go?!" I yell at her.

"No!" Screeching out for air, "please I have a son!"

My screams echoes against the wall so loud I don't give a fuck if the neighbors call twelve to this muthafucka. I disregard the few tears dropping down her face while I aim the strap at her dome.

Ignoring her cries I steady the nine right in the middle of her forehead. *Just hurry up and do it!* Loud voices scream over and over in my head. *Ahh! Do it! Get it over with! End it all!*

"Ahh!" Dropping the gun on the ground, "fuck! Fuck!

It's like a quick thought busts my skull wide open. *Then what?* Get up and go to work like nothing ever happened. Go to court to fight against the white man with my 'proper' words. Cover up the hate I feel for myself with nice suits.

My head drops to the floor.

I don't hate my career but how much shit I had to go through to get here. Now taking the life of a single mother to keep it all a secret is the last thing I want to do.

"Hermano, ha pasado tanto tiempo."

"What?" My head shoots up into the air, "it can't be."

The haze in my eyes shows only a long shadow standing in front of me. Whipping the blur away with my fists the first thing I see is black Timbs.

"Brother?" A raspy voice says, "what have you gotten yourself into?"

I can't believe my ears right now. I never been so happy to hear that stiff ass voice. And after half a decade I will never forget it.

"Hermano?" My back fell on the ground.

"Ace," he says, "I see you haven't changed a bit?"

Lifting my body up from the ground we exchange a short look at each other before throwing dap.

"Help me!" Alesha cries, "please help me."

I take one look in her direction, before my knees almost hit the ground.

"No!" Lethal blurts out. "You have to keep your head on my guy."

"No, no, no!" I shout out, "this shouldn't have happened. We have to take her home... w-we gotta..."

He cuts in. "And then what? I know you Johnathan, you aren't me... you lived by a code of honor. And this..." pointing at Alesha, "her, if she's laying on the ground in pain caused by you... she deserves it."

We stare into each other's eyes. One part of my mind faults me for involving a man like Lethal to clean up my mess, while the other grumbles at me to finish what I started. Protecting my life is way more important than anyone else's at this moment. No doubt Alesha made her bed, but for me to play a part in the Devil's work makes my stomach twist up in all kinds of knots of hopelessness. The life that once burned fire under my ass came knocking right at my door and I let it right in. Looking at Alesha's body withering away on the floor smacks me right back into the reality of my world. Proving me to be a menace to society that I am.

Pushing Lethal back, "no!" I speak up, "my name is Devine Staxx now and I am not going to make this girl's son motherless just because her feelings are hurt."

"And then what follador," poking my forehead, "ask yourself one question then 'Devine', why do you have a little perra laid out on your floor huh? You know she's going to call the cops on you soon as you let her go."

"No! Alesha pants the air, "I won't... please!"

I pace around in a quick circle. What the fuck! Shit! Why couldn't this girl just get some dick and go about her business? I will never understand these hoes man, one minute you want a niggah to just give you some good pipe then once you get this muthafucka you act like it's just all yours. I sit still, to be honest the real question that needs to be answered is who is her source of knowledge all in my past and shit.

"I did a lot of work to be untraceable," I say.

"Pshh, you don't think I know that" Lethal says, "I thought you were dead until I got an SOS text that I haven't seen in years..." looking back at Alesha, "but your main concern should be what we going to do with her."

Same old Lethal from back in the day, slice first, never ask questions later. This man is the coldest killer I've ever met in my entire 32 years. I've had my time where I did what I had to do to survive, nonetheless, when you meet someone who literally lives for shit like this, they are the most dangerous muthafuckas you will ever come across. I know a niggah like Lethal will never change, especially when he made it clear that he'll always eat, sleep, and breathe getting shit out the way.

Rushing up to Alesha I squat down to my knees, "if you tell me who sent you I will spare you." I say.

The blood rushing into her pupils threw me off. I care for her but not over the legacy I worked my ass off trying to build. I hope she takes this last chance into consideration to save her ass.

"If I tell you," tears fell from her eyes, "you have to let me go."

Lethal says, "Hermano, think about..."

Cutting him off, "chill out bro!"

Without hesitation she spills all the beans.

"He saw me sitting outside your house the other night," sucking in the air, "he said that if I told him what he wanted to know he would tell me who you really are!"

"What?!" I yelled. "Who... who told you that?!"

This niggah Javeon is playing a dirty game I see. Sending me in circles to get what he wants is low. I mean, it has to be him. What other man from my past knows all my dirty secrets except for...

"Drew," both Alesha and I say at the same time.

I take another look into Alesha's eyes, "fuck."

76

Breathing out another breath I raise back up to Lethal. Maybe he is right. If she can go low enough to meet up with a stranger to hurt me, who's to say she won't run straight to the police running her mouth.

My mind doesn't think of another reason to let her walk out of here breathing.

"Do it," my heart sinks into my gut, "make it quick."

"Si!" His face lights up, "todo estará' bien hermano," wiping his blade out of his pocket, "I'll make it quick."

"No!" Alesha screams out, "help! Please!"

"Sorry it has to be like this querido!"

In one twist of his wrist he slashes her throat. With her head in his grip, blood splatters all over his jeans then on my floor.

"Aww man!"

My stomach twists around in huge circles, trying my hardest not to throw my guts the fuck up. I can't stand to look at her body lying on the floor. Lifeless, open eyes.

What is life? I feel naive, ruthless, like nothing... A monster who will do anything to cover up the lies of my past I kept buried away for almost a decade. I managed to keep a low profile this long. As much as I hated to do it I had to nip this shit at the bud. Survive by any means necessary right?

All 32 of Lethal's teeth poke out from under his lips.

"Just like old times huh?"

I turn my head to him, "are you fucking serious right now bro?" I ask.

"Come on," he says, "I know a place where she can go."

I can't get my feet to take another step towards her body.

"Ace, bro." Putting her legs together, "you need to get a sheet and a garbage bag to put her body in."

I never knew how raw emotions can disturb any peace you have in your mind after staying away from a way of living for as long as I have. I want this bad dream to end. I wish I never met Lethal, Alesha, or Drew! None of this shit would be happening right now. I think back to the first time I touched a bag of dope. Oftentimes I wish I would've stuck to serving my granny friends, maybe I could have taken care of her instead of being in prison when she died. Maybe I could have been a good boyfriend to Trisha. *Maybe, just maybe.*

Three hours pass before we finish scrubbing my floor clean of any specks of Alesha's blood. I can remember the terrible stench of blood eating my damn nostrils up whenever we took somebody out. After wrapping her body up in a few sheets and garbage bags we hop into Lethal's truck on the side of the road.

"Eh, I will have one of my people get the stains out of your floor early tomorrow morning."

I keep my eyes out of the window.

"Si hermano, pick your lip up," he says, "this isn't your first rodeo and I'm sure it won't be the last, eh."

Turning my head to him I suck my teeth, "and why do you think that Lethal? Huh? Because I don't deserve to live a normal life."

"From what I witnessed so far I think you have been living a pretty sane life for this long my friend... and I also think by you summoning me here, that regular life you want to live is in jeopardy."

I should have handled my own damn business. I know Alesha was a pain in the ass, but something tells me I could have handled her in a different manner. By the time she rested in bed, she could have woken up in the morning with enough money to last her a lifetime. Instead, she's going to wake up to the heaven gates while her son wonders why his momma never came home.

Turning my head back out of the window, "you know what?" I say, "you're absolutely right as usual Lethal... I have some business that needs taken care of and enough money to put your pockets on Fat Joe."

"Ah," he smirks, "el cono que nunca me importó, I'm all for it."

"Bro, right now I really need you to speak in English. And slow this muthafucka down, you driving over 80 miles like we don't have a body in the trunk."

This niggah here boy. He never gave a fuck about anything. I see that didn't change at all. I blame myself, knowing the risks of hitting his line out of panic was not worth losing the tiny bit of sanity I hold on to for dear life. It's bad enough I still have to get up in the morning to see the mug on Javeon's ugly face. If I didn't want to hide under a rock a few hours ago I definitely do now.

Making a sharp turn into the trees his brakes screech a little bit as we run over a few rocks. We stop deep in some woods that I have never seen before. It looks like we fell into a deep abyss of the forest of no return or some shit.

"Brother, I know you are in pain," parking the truck, "but I am not your enemy. I'm not sure what you do but by the looks of your house you have made something out of yourself, and I am very proud of you for that, I just want you to make sure you aren't pretending to be something you are not."

"To be honest with you bro," with a hard sigh, "after hearing all those dudes' stories in prison who were innocent and shit I thought about being the one to help people like them prove their innocence," I say, "and ever since we took out Drew's brother I wanted to just start over... next thing you know I'm on the first bus to Cali."

I know Lethal and I may not ever see eye to eye. He is to this day one of my blood brothers or in his words his 'Hermano', even though we don't have the same mother. To be real I have a lot of pussy emotions going on right now. There's no telling how we can go about our future together. It would be nice to have at least one loyal person in my life to keep around.

Wishful thinking.

"Ah, si, so a lawyer?" Nodding his head, "that's sweet bro."

We catch up for a few more minutes.

"So one question before we handle business," I ask, "how the hell did you get into my house bro?"

We both laugh, knowing his crazy ass been breaking into houses way before we hit all those licks together. He even showed me a few tricks on how to not leave behind a trace of entrance.

Unbuckling my seatbelt, "I lowkey miss the old days man. Gambling, smoking, and don't let me forget all the pussy we used to pull," I say, "aye you remember ol' girl who claimed she didn't even like Mexican dudes."

"Yeah," he replies, "that was until she met me, and I put that ass in a hucklebuck."

"Shit," I burst out laughing, "man you stupid as hell dude, I never understood why you used to say that shit!"

"Because I'm a G youngin'," he looks at me, "and you are too hermano, you just have to get your life back in order... Devon" he laughs.

"Yo' it's Devine." I smack my lips, "man fuck you pussy... whatever."

Opening the door, "well come on now we can't sit here too long," he says, "I have another job in a few hours."

"Another job?" I ask, "don't tell me you do this for a living?"

I will never be surprised at this man's lifestyle. The only thing I ever worried about is if his thirst for blood would push him to cross me at any time. Although he never did, being a street niggah taught me to put nothing past no one. Mother, sister, brother, pappy, it doesn't matter who it is because at the end of the day everybody for themselves.

Opening his truck door, "tio, don't tell me you're judging me," he says.

He goes into his trunk pulling out two shovels and hands me one.

"Never mind my first question bro," holding onto the shovel, "let's just get this shit over with."

We drag her body deeper into the trees, stopping at what looks like some type of dead end. I look down into a dark pit that if you aren't careful enough to not trip into it yo' ass is finito. We start at the top then dig for almost an hour before getting the hole deep enough.

We jumped back up out of the hole to grab her body lying on top of the grass. *Damn.* Another thought comes... *This shit is really happening right now.* I'm rolling a lifeless body into a fresh ditch to rot inside of, only to wake up tomorrow like nothing ever happened. I don't know what it is about myself that I hate that much to allow myself to get this far but something has to change. I don't want to live in shame any longer. It's like the more I run away from my past the harder it comes busting down my door.

I look at the dirt for a few more minutes.

"Come," Lethal says, "we have to go now."

Disregarding all the torment fucking my insides up I get into the truck without a sound. Sad to say that I have more business to handle with Lethal. After tonight though I don't want to see another grave site in my life. There's no telling how her family is going to take her random disappearance. On the other hand I still have to make sure my name stays clean. I doubt that she told anyone about me in regard to our non- disclosure form, with her big mouth I have to make sure I double check so I can get rid of it all together.

"Just take me home," I blow out a huge breath.

He pulls back out of the woods, hitting the main road he presses his foot on the gas.

"Damn!" I shout, "slow yo' dumb ass down before we get pulled ov..."

'Woo-woo-woo-woo-woo'

"Aww fuck bro!"

Red and blue police lights flash in the back of our heads. This dumb muthafucka is about to get us fucked up for the rest of our lives. The officer behind us is going to have a field day with us. One look at a Mexican and black dude dressed up in all black covered in dirt, not to mention two fucking shovels in the trunk. *Oh!* This shit is fucking it! I can hardly breathe.

"Calm down tio," waving his hand in the air, "we are going to be just fine."

"What niggah?!" I yell again, "I told yo' dumb ass to slow the fuck down on these main roads now we getting blooped and shit..."

Steady speeding down the dark road he peeps back into the rearview mirror.

I shout, "stop! Niggah! What are you doing?"

"There's a steep cliff further down the road," he replies, "just in case we have to thump him and dump his ass."

His voice is too fucking calm for me. Me not knowing if I turned into a bitch out here or this man is the most fucked up person ever. I'm not taking out another muthafuckin' person tonight, especially not the police. At this point I'm praying just to make it back home to my bed.

"Are you fucking crazy?!" Yelling out, "stop this fucking car Lethal."

He looks out at the side of the road then presses down on the brake.

"Happy?" He asks.

I peek out the side mirror on my side at the police officer getting out of his car. Heading up to Lethal's side of the truck, his flashlight taps the window.

"Hello officer," Lethal says, "how can I help you tonight?"

The officer tilts his head while aiming the light right on our clothes.

"Do you know why I pulled you over?"

Lethal smiles, "I'm not sure but I know you're going to tell me."

I damn near punch this dude in his shit. Where does it stop? He has no chill whatsoever. He wants to sit and play with this man like we didn't just literally put a body 6 feet deep. If I don't make it back home tonight I can make one promise that Lethal is going to be in a grave next to Alesha's.

Both of his eyebrows rise, "license and registration," he says.

"Claro." Lethal replies.

Reaching over my lap he goes into the glove compartment.

"Here you go officer... Bryant," Lethal squints at his shirt.

Holding the flashlight steady on the dirt stains seeping into Lethal's pants.

"Mhm," the officer asks, "where you two coming from?"

Quickly cutting in, "yes, my sister lives over on Rodeo Drive," I say, "we just finished putting up a park for my niece."

"Mhm," the glare from the light hits my face, "hey, I know you... you own Clutch Case Law Firm, right?" He asks.

Sucking in some air, "yes," I reply, "we're right there on Atlantic Boulevard."

Great! Right up my fucking alley for this man to recognize me riding down the street in the middle of the night. Not only that I under no circumstances want Lethal to know where my place of business is located. I have to make it clear that he is not to make his way up in my shit at any cost. I will fuck him up if he plays with my hard work in any way. That goes for anyone. At the same time being seen with Lethal is bad for business, let's hope this officer doesn't make me flip his ass tonight because we all know what I am capable of when push comes to shove.

"Hang tight," focusing on Lethal's license, "Mr. Wright." Walking back to his car he jumps in.

Searching for the words to say to Lethal is an understatement. I'm rethinking everything in this moment, should I split on this niggah? Why did I ever think it was going to be different when he made it clear that he is who he is. In a way I think I'm just like him. Maybe I won't ever change either. We always say time will tell but in the end we never focus on the bigger picture.

Chapter 8

The Difference Between
Justice And Freedom

After it's all said and done in the end we're left to fend for ourselves. Ain't no telling how long before we both end up in a ditch of our own, plus the pressure of possibly having to take this officer out will be the end of my presence in this city.

"Mr. Wright?" I put the press down on Lethal's head, "you a whole fucking way. Are you trying to ruin my fucking life man?!"

"Calm down," swaying his hand, "you aren't the only one who can change his name."

Slamming my back to the seat, "oh jokes," I reply, "you are a fucking dickhead bro."

He's going to make my blood pressure high as hell. He takes nothing in life serious at all. Then again what can I expect from a serial killer who lives to literally take lives. The sole purpose of bringing this muthafucka into my life was to get this niggah Drew out the way, but no! I should have known some extra shit would drop right into my lap fucking with him.

Looking through his car I noticed a few shell casings lying on the back seat.

"Listen," his eyes focusing on the rearview mirror, "that ID expired a year back when I snagged it off this guy from my last job," he says, "now there's a ditch through those trees on our right side..."

"What?!" Cutting him off. "Why the fuck would you take another man's ID?"

"Oh I assure you he doesn't need it anymore." He goes on, "but when Officer asshole comes back to the car I want you to play like all is well to get his guard down before I snuff him with these..."

Grabbing a hold of some gold brass knuckles from under his seat almost takes me the fuck out.

I start to laugh, "then what foo"? We throw this white skinned police officer off a fucking ledge and drive his car to where, huh?" I ask, "through all these fucking trees?"

"No, we leave it here."

My face damn near drops onto my lap. I can't think of a single way out of this situation. Then again he didn't ask for my ID, this can probably give me some pull before Lethal gets us all killed.

"Just chill bro," I say.

Making his way back to the car I take a deep breath, lining my back up with the seat. If I couldn't get my thoughts in enough order to get us out of a simple traffic stop I promise to renege my own law license tomorrow morning. In this circumstance Officer Bryant is playing a hard bargain, in spite of that, he is a rookie in his field somewhere. Starting with him not asking for my identification can be used as a one up on our end. Either he needs a favor, or he holds respect for my crown.

"Alright, Mr. Wright, I am going to have to ask you to step out of the car."

"Woah, woah, woah," I cut in, "what seems to be the problem here officer?"

"Well it seems that Mr. Wright's license and insurance are both expired," answering with a sharp tone, "and it's kind of hard to believe that you two came from building a park at three o'clock in the morning... so I'm going to have to ask both of you to step out of the car."

Shit! If I don't think of a damn good comeback Lethal is going to cut the lights out of this dude with the quickness.

Gripping tighter on the brass knuckles, "alright officer," Lethal replies.

"No!" I push Lethal's back against his seat. "Being that you are simply going off of a hunch that we are guilty of any crime which is indeed not enough to stand for an objective credible reason indication," I say.

Officer Bryant takes a pause, "I understand but that does not explain Mr. Wright driving on both expired license and insurance," he replies.

"I do apologize for the inconvenience your officer, Sir," Lethal adds in, "but the park we just finished building for his sister is for the child we had together... so you can only imagine the amount of stress I am under. See I have all of my bills on autopay and when I switched banks I received new credit cards and must've forgotten to renew the autopay."

Officer Bryant hangs onto the window without a sound. I can tell that he's thinking about the non-benefits he'd receive for letting us go. I know that assessing performance in the police force holds a lot of weight in California. There can be a bright side to the end of this, I just have to sway any doubt holding his decision up.

"Officer Bryant," clearing my throat, "I see that your body cam is flashing green which indicates it's on standby mode, correct?"

We lock eyes.

I go on, "from my understanding being an officer in a big state where crime increased by 6 percent in only a year, who knows what pressure an officer can be under to keep himself protected."

Officer Bryant says, "so what are you implying Mr. Staxx? Because I definitely support the Black Lives Matter movement."

I return with a small smirk, "mhm, now we both know there's been at least 1200 'people' killed by the police in one year alone," I say, "there is no telling when you may need representation... and the way I see it, having one of the head of the top rated law firm in the state on retainer, free of charge, is a major plus on your end."

He stands there for a few without a sound. I just know he's about to try to take my black ass to jail then ship Lethal's ass back upstate to the penitentiary. I take another breath.

The second his flashlight turns off the constant beat in my heart slows down.

"Alright," he says, "here's your belongings Wright...you two have a good night."

"Yes Sir," Lethal takes his license back, "drive safe."

Backing away from the truck, "and I will be sure to keep your contact on hand Mr. Staxx."

"Sure thing," I nod.

Starting the car back up, Lethal pulls off.

"Woah man!" He laughs, "that was a rush aye."

I do not give a fuck about anything this man has to say, I want to go home. This has to be rated one of the most disturbing days of my life. I just want to go the fuck to sleep and wake up from this nightmare!

"Aww what's the matter Mr. Staxx," teasing me, "but no joke man, you have really made something out of yourself, huh?"

"Mhm-hmm."

It didn't take long to make it back to my house. The second we pull into my driveway I reach for the handle on the door.

"Uhm, so I needed your help finding Drew but seeing that he is closer than I thought it shouldn't be a problem finding him, right?"

"Hold up tio," he says, "if you want to take out your best friend, why didn't you do it yourself years ago?"

I keep my head facing the cars in my driveway.

"You, like I do, know the name of the game. When you do the dirt it comes back at you times ten," squeezing on the handle, "I just wasn't ready to deal with the consequences that come with the fallen pieces."

"Si," he says, "so moral of the story is if Drew comes out, your pretend life is over? And from the words of the bruja's mouth we just threw dirt over he is obviously running his."

Turning towards him, "I want him brought to me alive," I say, "and I will have your cash wired to your account the second you get that done."

The amount of trust I have for Lethal's locating skills will never be in question. Original plans involved us finding him together, but even being in the same room with him is a risk that I'm not willing to take. Back in the day I would have been ready to flush Drew's ass out, now I don't have it in me to spend hours scouring the streets for him. With him stalking my house it shouldn't take long for Lethal to find his location.

"One problem," he says, "what if he splits town now after not having contact with the girl?"

"He won't."

"And how are you so sure about this?"

"Because" getting out of the car, "he's planning to take the stand in one of my cases," I say, "I doubt he leaves town. He's trying to do me in."

Lethal nods his head.

He pulls off as I walk through my front door wasting no time making it to my room.

"Fuccck!," I fall out on my bed.

No words can explain the amount of irritation I feel. I don't have any thoughts either, I just want to go to bed.

A few weeks later I drag my feet into the courtroom. I take a look at the mug on everyone's face including Judge Rowling's. Guessing they're mad at my timing. I really don't give a fuck what any of them have to say at this point.

I head over to my counsel table right in the middle of Keisha's statement.

"They call him Spider because once he catches his victims there's no getting away," she explains, "a witness stated that he believes in no survivors and his venom is defined as viscous when he attacks."

Javeon's lips twists up, "niggah where da' fuck you been?" he grumbles.

Here this niggah go running his mouth.

"Mr. Staxx," Judge Rowling cuts in, "how nice of you to join us."

"Yes," I reply, "I am extremely sorry for my tardiness, your Honor I do not mean any disrespect to you or the Court."

I take a seat, keeping my eyes on the judge, Tristian hands over a copy of Javeon's motion of discovery.

"Mhm," he says, "just don't let it happen again," turning back to Keisha, "the Prosecution may proceed with it's argument."

Words can't be put together to explain the emptiness in my chest I woke up to this morning. Apart of me wanted to lay my ass back in the bed. Regardless of if I stayed home my bad mood was not going anywhere anytime soon.

"Mr. Staxx... Mr. Staxx," Judge Rowling's voice thumps my eardrum.

"Uh-uhm, yes," I speak out, "being that my client has never been convicted of any serious crime I find it difficult to perceive these allegations against him."

"Oh really," Keisha replies, "may the Prosecution present the court with evidence your Honor?"

"You may," Judge Rowling says.

"As I stated before there has been a various amount of reports against the defendant but the defendant has not been convicted," Keisha hands Bobby a photo, "in this photo this is the deceased body of one of the defendant's known street soldiers, Shawn Knowles, known by the street name Pent," turning to the jury, "he was brutally beaten and mutilated after betraying the defendant by running drugs through the east coast for another gang that goes by the name of Drummer Boyz, a very well-known drug organization and Mr. McCleaton's biggest competitors."

Pacing past the jury Bobby shows a picture of a bald dude hanging upside down by a rope tied around both his ankles with three bullet holes in the back of his head.

Bobby adds in, "let the jury please note that the victim has three children who are now without a father."

"Objection your Honor," I stand, "relevance."

"Sustained," Judge Rowling replies, "Miss Turner."

Keisha says, "apologies your Honor. Please let the jury disregard, however what my colleague meant to suggest is the very vile brutality of over 30 other victims elaborated by Mr. McCleaton's organization is a mere act of unhallowed behavior... and this is only what law enforcement has been able to gather," sucking in a breath, "there is no telling how many other victims that have gone undetected over the years that the case has been built against the defendant."

I try to flip through the motion of discovery quick instead all the words on this muthafucka are blurring together. I'm straight out of it on another level. *No please stop!* Alesha's little voice sounds off in the back of my head.

"Mr. Staxx." Judge Rowling repeats, "are you going to state your plea or continue to stare off into space?"

Forcing my head out of the clouds, "oh... uhh-uhm, excuse me your Honor, I'd like to point out the transgression of not receiving the motion of discovery in time enough to prepare my argument your Honor."

Without looking over to Keisha I can feel the bright smile she's working up on her face.

"Yes, yes it is very transgressional on your behalf," Judge Rowling responds, "and you know what else it is, it's very unprofessional for you to come into my courtroom late without a clue Mr. Staxx... I'd strongly advise you to have all of your ducks in a row," his lips twist, "but I indeed agree, this trial continues next week," thumping his gavel down, "court is adjourned."

I'm gone get her ass, watch. Holding onto my strong posture I keep my head high. This is a prime example of rule number 5 when you're a black man in America... never let them see you down even when you really fucked up. Even with zero words spoken I can comprehend the glare going across Javeon's face. He wants to go upside my head like a muthafucka.

On the flip side of how bad everything looks right now; we still have a great advantage with his motion of discovery now that it's in my hands. Not bypassing the kind of power I have to find the most buried secrets of whoever I see fit at the time. If Tristian did his job right I'll have Keisha's sweet lips kissing my tip again in no time.

"Hey, hope everything is okay," Bobby smirks, "you seem a little tired."

I throw back a soft smirk while Tristian and I head out of the courtroom.

"Hey, you did what I told you to do, right?" I ask Tristian.

"Yes and you won't believe what I found out Sir."

Sparks light up half of my soul. My team never fails to get me what I need. I took a chance depending on Tristian to take on a job this big so fresh in the game. Something tells me that he can handle more than he's aware of. Matter of fact I know it.

We get back to the office. Leading him straight into my office, he shuts the door behind him.

Taking a seat behind my desk I get right to the point, "so what do we have?"

"So it turns out that our friend Miss Turner hasn't had the best of luck when it comes to her financial situation."

"What?"

"Yes," he takes a seat, "we don't have much to go on at the moment... however her home has been under great threat of being foreclosed if she doesn't come up with enough to catch up on her mortgage."

Mhm. Looks like Miss Keisha is on her last limb of hope to save face. In situations like these it makes more sense that she is fighting to keep her name if anything. Still, I need more information if I am going to make deals on the back end. She is the type of woman who you need to flush out in every aspect. Suffocating any options of argument before you corner her is the way I need to go if I am going to walk away with another W under my belt.

I flop the motion of discovery over on the table.

"Did they say anything else?" I ask him.

"No Sir," he blinks, "no-not at the moment... they said they're going to get back to me with more information. Was I supposed to press them," stuttering, "d-do you want me to call them back."

Waving my hand, "hey, calm down," I say, "you are doing great kid... keep up the good work."

He smiles, "thanks Sir."

"No problem. Now if you don't mind I have to make sure I build a solid case if we're going to win this trial."

The way I see it is in some way Bobby is holding something over Keisha's head. And being the stupid muthafucka he is, I doubt he's handling anything but a hamburger on his own. I need to gather more information on both their asses. Oh yeah, if they think they did a big one today I can't wait to see the stupid look on both of their faces when I blow the whole little operation up.

Running my finger down each page of the discovery, I pass a few grand jury transcripts, I notice a lot of this bullshit was thrown together by the statements made by a few familiar names named as the defendants and co-defendants. Sad to say it's a few of these niggahs Javeon allegedly took out, like that lil niggah Pent she mentioned in court today. I used to always see him riding down 14th street with the Opps who ran with the Drummer Boyz, which tells me that Keisha has some of her facts right. *Shit.* I scan to the expert witness section and don't see Drew's name. *This can't be right.* In fact, there is one out of three witnesses that I don't know in this case. Whoever Roshaun Cole is, I can find out with the snap of a finger.

An ignorant lawyer would look at this and not know any better, bad to say for Keisha I'm not the one. She can play her pity card on the jury to get her way with those other niggahs. But I'm going to bury her ass in court now that I have my play on her. I can use it to sway her argument.

Knock. Knock.

"Excuse me boss," Tristian walks in, "you have someone here to see you."

My heart pounds against my chest hard as fuck. Peeking down at my phone I see a few missed calls from an unknown number. I just know this dumb muthafucka Lethal didn't make his way to my shit. God, I'll floor this niggah right here right now.

"Tell them to go away," I grumble.

"And then you wouldn't be able to enjoy the good company of a Queen."

I jump out of my chair the second I got a hold of that graceful voice sending chills down my spine.

"Radiance," tugging on my collar, "what are you... I mean how did yo-you, how are you?"

Damn she got a niggah all kinds of flustered. Among other things she is still the most beautiful woman I have ever met in my life. I can hardly think whenever she's around, still that doesn't mean I always let myself show it.

Tristian says, "well I'll just leave you two alone."

"Hey!" I stop him in his tracks, "uhh-uhm, leave the door cracked."

Radiance smiles as I gain back my composure.

"Take a seat," pointing to the chair across from my desk, "let's talk."

She sits down, "so I was on my lunch break and one thought came to mind when I walked past that old sandwich place we used to always go to."

"Mhm," I smirk, "Jackson Place. You used to get a turkey sandwich no mayo"

"Yeah," smiling back, "and you used to get your ham sandwich with everything but tomatoes."

Aww man. It slipped my mind how much fun we used to have. I remember how spending every second of every hour with this woman filled my life up with purpose. As a result of having good faith deep inside my mind I understood the value of having a good woman on your side. Radiance's name describes her good fortune in all aspects of life. She was the bright spot in my life.

"So that's it?" I ask, "that's what brought you down here?"

While she reaches down into her purse I scope out the red lipstick on her lips. *Mhm.* Her sexy ass knows how to turn a niggah on without doing anything at all. I can tell that her skin is so soft too, by the brightness of her milk chocolate skin.

"I got you this," handing me a paper bag, "I thought you might be hungry."

Unwrapping the paper to a ham sandwich I put it back into the bag.

"Thank you so much for this," I throw out a tiny smirk.

Not to be a dick about it but this woman came into my life at the wrong time. There's no way I can fit in any time for fun, not even a little bit of it. I'm surrounded by killers, drug dealers, and professional liars. Not to mention sometimes having to be one out of the three. I can ruin her life.

"Hey uhm, if you don't mind I have to get back to work."

"Oh, uhm... sure," she replies.

She heads for the door.

It's in her best interest to steer clear of a niggah like me. The younger version of me craved a getaway, but that would put her in grave danger. When I didn't know any better I allowed myself to get attached to her grace in every way possible. Now she deserves to be happy, therefore hanging around a muthafucka that only killed a woman half her age less than a few weeks ago. I'll be doing her a solid.

"Hey," turning around, "I really came by hoping to get some of your advice on a few contracts I'm drawing up for my new building."

"Oh yeah," I say, "I forgot... congratulations."

I sit and contemplate for a second. If I keep it strictly business with her I can send her about her way with no problems. Then again, I'll be a fool to believe that I can see her fine ass walk away from me. On the other side of it all, it's nothing that she hasn't done before. Somewhere in my life I need to get a sense of some type of self-control around her. I mean, I have the act down packed like a muthafucka, it's how I really feel every time we are apart. I can't even get her out my head.

"Uhm... sure," I reply to her, "let's have a look."

Coming back to my desk she slaps both her hands down.

"Well, you know what? I left them back at my office, so it looks like you'll just have to come with me for a quick second."

"I don't think that's a good idea," my eyebrows raise, "I have a lot of work to do and..."

Chapter 9

Never Say The Word 'Can't'

"Aww come on workaholic," cutting me off, "it won't be long. And maybe you can eat your sandwich."

Her fingernails squeeze around the sleeve of my suit until we make it outside.

I don't see her car parked anywhere so I'm assuming her office is nearby.

"You walked here?" I ask.

"Yup," she smiles, "I'm right around the corner. What? Don't tell me you're worried about scratching the snake skin off of your shoes."

"Oh funny," I laugh.

What I liked most about her is the soft sense of humor she carried. She always had a knack for bringing light to any situation. We pace up the street past a few lights and around a steep corner to a strip with only a few big buildings in the parking lot. Stopping at the first building the big sign on the door in purple reads *Rose*

Gold Sculpting. Going into her shop she cuts the lights on then goes to set her purse on the desk in a back room.

"Wow," I say, "it looks really good in here."

I look around at the decor of the building. Just like the purple sign out front the walls match a few purple and black chairs sitting at the front desk which is most likely where her secretary will sit. She's really outdone herself. I'm glad the one dream she always talked about came true.

"So, do you like it?"

Still glancing around, "I love it."

She smirks back, "thank you, well here's the forms."

Handing over a tan folder I take a seat to flip through the pages.

"Mhm, are these the contracts you are going to have your assistant sign?"

"Yes, I want to give whoever I choose a chance to be under me but still have the freedom to take on other jobs while working for me."

"So you still want them to remain a 1099 employee?"

"Yes," she answers.

"And you are aware that you can still pay yourself from the company's income, but that pay is not tax-deductible, right?"

Turning over a few more pages I see that she is giving the company a time limit to run, which is a little strange to me. Most people file LLC's when they first startup to save the headache of filing taxes under an EIN number instead of their social security number.

"Are you sure you want to go this route?"

Taking the folder out of my hand she throws it on the floor.

"Yes," she says.

My head lifts up to the sound of her pulling down the zipper on her dress.

My throat gulps. "Wh-what you doing girl?"

She jumps on my lap and starts kissing my forehead, then my nose, leading down to my lips, her hands rubbing on my dick.

This was a clear setup, whole time she wanted to get me all alone to try to rape a niggah. And as much as I want to let her do her thang I can't get myself caught up in no more shit right now.

"Mhm," I groan at the sweet smell of flowers, "baby?"

Our lips connecting together back to back led to our tongues exchanging all types of spit. Next thing I know my pants on the floor while squeezing on a handful of ass at the same time. Her voice whispers into my ear, 'ouu you don't know how much I missed you daddy.'

Fuck. I missed her too much too. No doubt the last seven years she crossed my mind from time to time. I can't count the number of times my dirty ass mind imagined us making love. How many times I wanted to stick my fingers deep inside her pussy and make her suck the juices off of them. This girl has always been the one thing I regretted letting walk out of my life because I wasn't man enough to not let her go.

"Wait, wait," pulling my head back, "baby we can't do this right now."

Forcing her lips back up to mine.

"Uhh," she huffs the air, "it's okay baby just go with the flow."

Her pussy grinds on my dick making this muthafucka solid as hell.

Fuck it. I squeeze harder on her hips rubbing my dick up against her panties. This woman doesn't know how crazy she drives me. She the type to have you sitting outside her house with a gotdamn beatbox playing 'whatever you want'. No lie, I want her bad as fuck. I'll do whatever she needs me to do for her. I'll be whatever she needs me to be. Even if that means making the hard ass decision to be a gentleman, and not beating her shit up in the middle of her cold ass shop.

"Baby, baby!" I blurt out, "we can't do this here."

"Wait," she pulls back. "Well, why not? You seeing someone else?"

I clutch my fingers onto her chin, "no," with a smug look, "I just don't want..." Snatching away she gets up to put her dress back on.

"You don't want to what Devine? To be in a relationship?"

Aww shit. I forgot how sensitive she can be when her stubborn ass doesn't get her way.

"No, baby," jumping out of the chair, "listen," blowing out a breath, "I want you."

"Yeah right."

"No for real, I missed you more than you know since you left," I pause, "it's just... let me take you out first."

"Well, I don't..."

"Come on baby just let me do this one thing right."

The frown on her face turns into a big grin. I knew if I came at her the right way this time she would give me a chance to make up for all the years we missed being together.

If she lets me, I promise to show her the best sites in the city. Whether she wants to go out on my yacht, jet, or a walk on the beach I promise to make it the best night of her life. And after if she wants me to knock a few screws loose I can do that too.

"Let's go," she says, "It's getting dark out and I don't want your balls to shrivel up in this cold ass building."

Throwing my pants back on I return with a nod.

"Yes ma'am."

We make it halfway to my building before the sun almost reaches its peak.

I stop, "hey it's getting late I can have my driver take you back."

She replies, "oh no," checking out the sky, "I'm good here."

"Baby, it's dangerous out here and I would lose it if anything happened to you. Let me get you back to..."

She cuts in with a peck on my cheek, "it's okay," she laughs, "I'm a survivor, and if anyone jumps out of the cut I'll use that one karate move that you like."

"Radiance," twisting my neck, "let me take care of..."

Taking a few steps backwards, "welp I'll see you in a few days... 8' o clock?" She asks.

I stand in the middle of the sidewalk trying my best to hold myself back from throwing her ass over my shoulders.

"Radiance." I call out. "Radiance."

She puckers her lips out while blowing me a kiss before she continues back towards her shop.

I see this woman hasn't changed one bit. Although it fucks my head up every time. I find that shit sexy as hell. I love a woman with her own mind. Following her own instincts still letting me beat that shit up until her legs shake all uncontrollably.

I watch her fat ass switch from side to side until she disappears at the corner.

I'll let her do her thang today. And in a couple days she'll be doing her thang by my side. I want to take my time with her. Usually a woman who knows how to handle her own is a dangerous woman if her intentions aren't good. My baby is nothing but good though. She proved that a long time ago.

In the process of making my way back to the firm my stomach twists in small knots thinking about how close we were to making a baby. I think about where I'm going to take her. Only the best for my lady.

A few minutes away from my building and I feel a bold shadow coming up behind my back full force. I don't know what to think. The only thing that comes to mind is Javeon has his people about to put me in a body bag. *Fuck!* Not that I had to walk around with a strap on my waist in years but I'm never the type to get caught slipping. On top of that I don't remember the last time I took a stroll down the damn street either. I hope they didn't follow my baby back to her place of work. I instantly regret leaving out with her. If I put her or her place of business in harm's way I'll hate myself more than I already do.

With both my fists cocked in the air I turn around, "what the fuck?!"

"Aye' calm down hermano, it's just me."

I huff at the air, "damn bro! What are you doing following me and shit?!"

A sense of relief hit my spine with it being Lethal instead of one of Javeon's soldiers.

He cocked both his hands in the air mimicking me, "woah, you expecting someone else to run up on you or something?"

"No, dickhead," I reply. "I just don't like people walking all up on me and shit."

"Then you need to strap up man, especially if you're going to walk up the street, no need to be naked."

Twisting my eyes, "what is it that you want?" I ask, "you found something on Drew?"

Despite not having a clue how long he's been on my trail, a part of me is happy he didn't make his way inside of my building. I answer to no one, still, the last thing I need is nosey employees asking questions.

I lead him into a cut to get out of plain sight.

"So, hermano. I know we have been apart for some time now, but you know like I know we've never lied to each other."

Here we go. I'm not stupid nor is Lethal, there ain't no telling what kind of digging he's done. I had high hopes that he just did his job, instead he wants to follow me around to be all in my business. *Damn!* He doesn't know Radiance at all, so I know he's going to be on my case about her.

Most things never change, first thing he's going to swear is she's going to throw me off track. The truth is he doesn't need to be in any of the business that don't make his pockets fatter.

I ask with a straight face, "what are you talking about?"

"I'm talking about the fact that you're representing that woo-ha Spider," twisting his fingers, "that motherfucker is one of the biggest drug lords to originate out of Ohio man," easing closer, "not to mention the hottest."

"Look I know bro, I..."

He cut in, "Look, I understand that you raised him since yay-high, aye, put him in the game," tapping my chest, "but if you wanted to bring me in you should have warned me that his men would be cruising in the streets here man."

I know Lethal, he's asking questions, that only means he has gotten in some trouble with Javeon or one of his people I don't know about. I'm damn sure of the severity because the main rule in Lethal's handbook is to never ask questions. I guess that's how he keeps his emotions intact.

Easing up on him, "look bro, things change just how people change... mhm, and the way I see it the boy I showed how to beat the system died a long time ago, Spider is just another check, one that keeps my pockets fed so I can make sure to keep all this shit rolling."

He stares into space for a few minutes. I didn't expect him to dig deeper into the job, something doesn't seem right about this. I can play it cool, but I might have to pay more attention to his actions from here on out. I doubt that he's working with Javeon, despite that he can be making plans on the side. I learned that Lethal always has an extra trick up his sleeve. No question that he loves me to death, but we learned a long time ago that that quote 'every man for themselves' goes harder in the streets.

With a hard sigh, "aight hermano," patting my shoulder, "I can tell you what I found, but it's not much."

Finally, the key to ending all of this madness. Now I can think about all the places I am going to take my sweet Queen when all this is over. Her fat ass bouncing in a bikini on my yacht, or her pretty ass hands caressing mine in the jet while we're in the air looking down at the city lights didn't sound too bad. Words can't explain how much I ache to go back to my regular routine, and to add Radiance to the mix is going to be fucking divine.

"So I have a few colleagues down here who can trace a motherfucker down with the snap of a finger, right?"

"Okay," I reply. "So what'd they find bro? Anything we can use?"

He pauses for a second, "no... however when they ran his name through their system they didn't find a trace of this guy, I mean nada."

Fuck. I have to let him know the truth about the entire situation at hand. Being a lawyer can get you out of a bunch of shit at the same time his balls gon' drop when I do. That mere voice inside my head hopes he can understand the severity of my life on the line if we let Drew get on the stand.

"There's more you need to know about," clearing my throat, "well, when the girl admitted to talking to Drew it wasn't just any coincidence that he was stalking my house."

He blinks a few times, "okay, well, what does that mean?" He asks, "he's after you because he found out we smoked his brother, isn't he?"

Man. This is a hard conversation to have. When I let him know that Drew is involved with the Feds he's going to lose his shit. I hope I don't have to fuck this man up. I understand that I'm wrong for lowkey moving sloppy, but regardless of that you just can't tell him everything. Besides, there's only one person I trust with my whole life, Radiance.

Rubbing my hand across my face, "I just found out a few days ago..." I huff at the air.

"Found out what follador... spit it out eh'."

I step back to prepare myself to put my hands up.

"He may be sneaking out, but I'm pretty sure our old friend Drew is in witness protection."

Don't get me wrong, I said this before I will never fear a man no matter how big, small, off the rails he is, except a dude like Lethal is the most predictable, unpredictable man in the world.

Crossing his arms over each other, "oh," he says.

Waiting for the other ball to drop I'm more than shocked at his reaction. I may be even stunned by it if I'm being honest.

I go on, "so with your people having access to the system I'm assuming they are..." *Pow!*

Lethal's fist goes right across my right cheek.

"En qué coño me ha metido tu estúpido culo, eh?!"

Clutching both my cheekbones I bend over then spit out some blood.

"Bro what the fuck?!" I yell out.

"There is no secret that I don't give a fuck about the cops tio," shaking his hand, "but the Feds Ace?"

Charging at him my head hits him right in the stomach.

"Fuck you!" I yell out. "You stupid fuck!"

Both our backs smack the ground. He jumps on his knees then slams his elbow into my stomach.

"Ahh!" I shout, "you pussy."

Gasping out in the air he recovers his balance on his feet.

This fucking dickhead! I curl up holding my stomach trying to stop the pain. It feels like one of those hoes really cut my balls off this time.

Pow! I lift up just enough to bop his dumbass right in the balls.

Dropping to his knees with both his hands holding his shit. "Ahh!" He yells.

"How that feel pussy!" I cough.

I fell back to the ground.

Missing a whole month at the gym hit different when you've aged a couple years. The reality of it all is that he had to get a few hits off. We haven't had a chance to politic on my disappearance, on top of me hitting his line when I need something. I get it. I can also put my feet in his shoes. At the same time this is my brother, we fight, we joke around, but at the end of the day I know he's going to make it happen regardless of our mishap tonight.

We lay on the ground side to side finding the breath in our lungs.

"Look bro," I say, "I know you feel some kind of way that I dipped without letting you know, then I hit your line with my Fed problem and don't tell you. But I assure you that you are one of the most solid, Latino mixed with black, white and a pinch of psycho friend that I have ever had."

"You remember the first time I called you Hermano?"

"Yeah, when we knocked ol boy screws loose in the joint for trying to take your pop tarts."

"Yes, Hermano-brother," he replies. "Which means we're in this for life man".

I look back at him for a few seconds, "I honestly feel that way too bro."

Keeping his head up at the stars, "mhm... and you are the dumbest realest friend I've had chico."

Without seeing his face I recognize the high pitch tone in his croaky ass voice. Telling me this scrap session needed to happen a long time ago. Matter of fact I was overdue for an ass whoopin' in his defense.

We help each other off the ground then dap up.

"Alright," I say, "so I was saying that with your people having that king of access to the system they have to be the police, right?"

"Well, sort of, they are retired police, but I prefer not to have him in a mix-up with the Feds."

"What? Well, why the fuc... why not?"

If it's not one thing it's another. Now, this dude is holding back resources that can end all my problems. I'm so tired of all the bullshit going on in my life. This shit makes me feel like a prissy bitch or something.

"You know it's not like that dio, calm down a minute."

Getting closer to him my teeth bit down on my lip.

"Then what is it like? Huh? Because it seems like to me you're fucking around with my life on the line."

He pushes me back, "it's my son," his voice hardens, "and if I would've known this woo-ha, Drew, is a big ass rat I would of did it my way... that's why from now on you need to tell me everything."

His son? I need to step back for a second...he is right to a certain extent. I am man enough to admit my wrongs. I in no way, shape, or form would ever put my life over his son's. But first, I can't wait to hear what woman was crazy enough to pop out one of his kids. He has to be at least in his late twenties, not to mention being 'retired', which I doubt. Fucking around with Lethal's ass he probably got him into some mess to get him kicked off the force.

"Oh bro, congratulations," I tease, "who's this lucky lady I'm sure to meet soon."

"She's deceased." he says quickly, "anyways it's getting too late, and I don't want to be seen out by one of Spider's men... I'll phone you as soon as I get hands on Drew."

Assuming I struck a nerve I give off a quick nod before we walk off in different directions. Although I have no room to judge his situation when mine is sure as hell nowhere near better. I have plenty of questions that need answering from my old pal. Right now, making it back home to gather my thoughts is more important. No need to worry, if anyone is going to handle what needs to be done I can count on Lethal a hundred percent.

My driver rolls up right on time to swoop me up from in front of my building. I have him take a few shortcuts to get me home faster so I can plan for my baby's perfect date.

"See you tomorrow," my driver let me out the car.

"See you tomorrow," I reply.

After I get into the house I go off course of my usual routine, instead I head into the living room to catch up on a few of my favorite shows.

"Alexa, go to the Power universe."

Now that I think about it that niggah 50 really did his thang. From running the streets to whacking the white man's pockets a million times over is what I aim for daily. It's one thing to change your life and another to shift it. Most times I think back to all the terror I inflicted on others because I was in pain. That shit doesn't ever go away. All the blood spilled, bodies dropped, Drew don't even know how sorry I am that I took away the one person he loved most in the world. If I knew what I know now I would spare any person who has a chance to live their life the way they want.

Chapter 10

Stand For Nothing;
Fall For Anything

To live it. It wasn't until Alesha's last breath that I understood Mr. Robert's meaning of not having the right to take another's life into your own hands. That shit haunts me. No one on earth deserves to die, in my opinion look at me... I praise Jehovah every day that I got to make it out of the trenches alive.

A few hours into Power Book 2: Ghost and I'm cracking up at the lil niggah Tariq for running around late for school. In a way that used to be me. I relate to his character a lot. Doing what I had to do to survive. Taking shit down at an early age. The only difference is I wasn't as smart as he was at the age of 18. It wasn't until I found myself in a jail cell learning all that I could in the Law's Library.

Knock. Knock.

"Who the fuck at my house at this hour?"

Pausing the TV, I look at the time which says it's a couple minutes from 2 in the morning.

Did Lethal find Drew and bring him to my house? Then again, he has way more polish than to do that dumb shit.

I rush into my room, grabbing my strap from out the drawer I ease up to the doorway. Blowing out a few breaths I press my eye up to the peephole...

Man damn! What does this muthafucka want? I damn near take out four niggahs punching the air while I rush my shit back in the drawer. *Aight. Just get this shit over with.* I talk myself out of pretending I'm not here as I make my way to open the door.

I crack open the door, "what's up?"

"Damn niggah, I know you heard me at the door." Keisha damn near breaks the muthafucka down.

I back up, "damn girl why are you busting all in my shit like that?"

"Because you acting like you can't answer the phone... what? You got another bitch in here or something?!"

Looking at the couch I must've forgotten to take my phone off silent. In the midst of her crackly ass voice throwing a fit I rush to it making sure I didn't miss a call from my baby. All I see is 30 missed calls from Keisha.

"Fuck," looking at my home screen.

Following in my footsteps, "yeah," twisting her hands in the air, "because you been acting all crazy like you don't know."

What is this lady talking about? I'm so sick of bitches feeling like they can pop up at my shit.

I flop down on the couch.

"What do you want Keisha?"

"You already know what I want Devine."

The last thing I really need is to put another muthafucka in the dirt. I don't even feel like being bothered by her or anyone. Matter of fact if she ain't bringing me any information to get the upper hand in the case which I doubt, then she can leave me the fuck be.

"I know you want me," she says, "I see how you be looking at me in court, but you want to act all stubborn like you don't miss this wet ass pussy."

Oh. So that's what this pop up visit's about... that's something I wouldn't have had a problem helping her with a few days ago. Now that my wife is coming back into my life there's no way in hell I'm fucking that up.

Waving my hand at her, "pshh, do we be in the same courtroom?" I ask.

Pushing her body up against my head, her hands rub across my waves.

"Mhm, yeah we do," lowering her voice, "and you know you want it so stop lying to yourself."

Aww shit is all I can say. Every time I give a female some of this good pipe they think they own this muthafucka. Last time I checked my guy Big John belongs to one person only, and it's not these quick fucks or easy pussy's.

Most of these women are disposable. In a sense they have no self-esteem or issues that they can't handle. I have a list of women on speed dial. I can get pussy anytime I want. Any hour of any day if I make the call they coming. I don't have time for that, nor do I want it.

"Look, pushing her hands down, "I have to get up in the morning so..."

She jumps onto my lap, "you're not the only one who has a job Devine," she says, "besides I need you to take my mind off the boatload of work that dropped on my desk about your assistant this morning."

What she mean the work about my assistant? *Be cool bro.* I repeat to myself. If I show her any sign of unease she gone automatically assume the worst. Last thing I need is her up my ass about some bullshit. The best thing for me right now is to play the game with her. I may regret what I have to do. Sadly, that's how it goes.

Pulling her in closer, "mhm," our lips connect, "my ex assistant? What happened to her?"

"Oh you didn't know?" She asks. "Her mother reported her missing this morning when she didn't come back to get her baby boy."

I throw out a fake sigh, "oh damn... well I let her go a few days ago, she's had a lot of complaints about her behavior at the job and I had to let her go," I say, "I hope she's okay."

We look into each other's eyes.

"Yeah, well I'm sure she's fine," rubbing my nuts, "enough of that though."

"Yeah," I agree, "I'm 'bout to give you what you been missing."

Throwing her back to the couch my body lays on top of hers. Right after we tongue each other down I go in for the kill. Dragging her pink Victoria Secret panties down to her ankles, my lips peck inside of both her thighs.

"Uhh! Yes daddy swallow that pretty muthafucka."

I flip her on her stomach then shove my dick right between her legs.

"Ahh! Uhh! Yes daddy," she screams.

It's getting harder to focus on some pussy I already had at the same time as trying to push the thoughts out of my head about Alesha's motherless son. On top of wanting to save this dick for someone who deserves it, which is my babygirl. I can play nice to get what I want tonight but I meant what I said when things are about to change, quick too.

"You like that?!"

I pump faster and faster to get every extra reaction out of her that I can. Her legs gone hurt so bad in that morning that all the niggahs in the office gone know she got her brains blown out the night before.

I slap her fat ass cheeks then roll her over on her side.

Her little voice moans again, "fuck me daddy!"

"Oh you want this dick deep in you, huh?" With a tear falling out of her eye, "yes... I want it!"

Rubbing my tip up against her clit.

"Say please," I tease her.

I play too much; she likes that shit though. Women love when you make them squirm. Keisha is the type of woman who loves to beg, plead with a niggah to get what she wants. I think because she has all the power to do what she wants in the prosecution's office that she craves for a man that tells her what to do. If you really think about it, looking at the amount of people who work corporate jobs, you see that most people want to be told what to do because they don't know what to do.

"Please" Screaming loud as hell, "please put it in me daddy!"

My pipe squeezes right through her tight hole.

"Uhh!" She yells.

Lowering my voice, "shut up."

Pumping faster and harder I focus on this big ass nut I feel about to bust.

"Damn girl," I whisper.

Without another word I snatch my shit out following with a lump of nut pumping out on both her ass cheeks.

"Yes!" She moans.

"Damn," I drop on my side.

We lay there, our shallow breaths colliding. With her still on her side my mind goes back to the inner space clouding it. Full of raging flames that I can't seem to get rid of. Is it the same anger that took the life of that girl, or the hate that I felt for myself since a jit?

I don't even know.

Her voice rings in my eardrums. "Damn niggah are you good?"

"Huh, what, yeah... yeah, why you ask that?"

"Because you're spacing out again. Don't tell me you're thinking about your little thot again."

"I'm not bab..."

"And where's my towel?" She cuts in, "ugh! You've been acting real weird!"

Here this bitch go acting like she don't have an ounce of sense. This shit is one of the reasons why I don't fuck with women who didn't have a dad in they life. They don't know how to hold themselves together like ladies. All this spazzing out to get a reaction out of me which she not about too. I'm about to give her all types of fantasies to live off of.

I stand up, "calm down baby sheesh, I'll go get you a towel."

Almost running to my bedroom I grab a towel out of the bathroom closet. *Man.* It's always the ones you don't want that do too fucking much. After this case I'm gone cut this hoe straight off like she died. Matter of fact I'm cutting everybody the fuck off. To think I disappeared from Ohio without a trace, these folks ain't saw nothing yet.

I head back into my living room.

"Cause what bitch you had up in here Devine?!"

Keisha standing in the living room straddling Alesha's jacket around her fingertips.

116

I'm stuck in the doorway.

I'm five seconds away from snapping on this bitch and throwing her ass out.

"What?! It's not even like that..." I rush up to her.

"Then what's it like Devine?!" She yells.

Throwing on her panties before sliding on her pants she smacks the jacket across my face.

"Fuck you! Fuck the bitch you fucking! And I don't ever want to see your lying ass face again!"

I stop for a second. We went through this before, she gets mad, assume she knows what the fuck she's talking about, next thing she's at my door in expensive ass lingerie. Out of all my years I have more than enough experience to pick up on attention seeking bimbo broads. What she really needs to be worried about is the way I'm about to fuck up that career. I'm sick of these hoes.

"You know what?" I say, "go ahead, since you don't want to listen to me when I don't have a single reason to lie to yo' dusty, mediocre pussy having ass hoe."

Her mouth drops to her chest. "What?!"

"Yeah," walking her to the door, "and you can say bye to that reputation because like that trash ass pussy you got your career is about to be just like it."

Almost ripping the door off its hinges when I open it, I slam that muthafucka right in her sad ass face.

Fuck her. She, like everybody else, means nothing to me at this point. I'm not about to keep explaining myself to them either. They can all get on their knees to suck my dick.

Not even cutting my TV off I jump right into my bed. All I see is the need to be alone. No one bothering me is a blessing in disguise that I'm all for. Being able to take time to figure myself out is the best thing to happen for me. For the first time in ten years I admit before I knock out... I'm tired.

In the morning I open my eyes to the sun beaming on my face.

"Man fuck this shit today." I say.

You ever want to say fuck the world to only worry about yourself? That's how I feel today. I turn back over in my bed. All I want to do is go to sleep for however long I want too. Shit, I have the money to do that.

After hours in bed I watch the sun hit its peak... Next thing I know I'm back at the office a week later twisting around in circles in my chair. What is there to do when the one thing you want to do is be back home in bed. It doesn't help that my baby hasn't called either. She knows how to keep a niggah wondering. What has she been doing? Where has she been? I kept enough composure to not pop up at her place of work. In spite of that she still could have hit my line to tell me that she is at least doing okay. Not that she needs help getting her business together, it would've been a great feeling to hear about it.

The old me would have spazzed out, instead the promise I made to myself a few days ago is going to stick. Well, at least until I figure out what I'm going to do with Drew ass. Going behind my back to snake me with a female was a pussy move on his end. Anyways, he'll be taken care of soon enough.

Buzz. Buzz. Buzz. Buzz.

My phone vibrates in the left pocket of my suit.

Yes! Thinking to myself. It has to be Radiance! Taking it out of my pocket I see a no caller ID across the screen. *Shit.* Who is this? It might be Javeon having one of his people hit my line. I haven't went to see his ass in days. And the way I dogged Keisha's desperate ass I know she's going to do everything in her power to ruin both him along with me. Or it could be Lethal telling me he finally found Drew. Either way, I have to pick up the phone to face the repercussions of whoever is on the other end of the line.

"Hello." I say.

"Uh-uhm, yes Mr. Staxx."

"Yeah, who is this?"

He says, "this is Tom in Michigan, we did business when Sam was out of the office last time."

Straightening my back up against the chair. "Oh! Oh! Yes, how are you?" I ask.

"I'm good, I actually wanted to apologize for getting Sam's message late to reach out to your assistant about a Miss. Turner."

The first thing that comes to mind is the way I'm going to fuck Tristian up for lying to me. The second thing is that if he didn't talk to my girl Sam or this dude to get the information he gave about Keisha, who is he screwing on the opposite team that knows all that about her? Damn sure her problem isn't in public records. Was he telling the whole truth? One thing for sure is I'm gone get to the bottom of the whole situation.

I play it cool.

"Oh no problem at all, I know things get messy."

"Right," he says, "so great news is we have a ton of information on her that I dug up for you at the moment, but with that, the way the casino has their system protected we have to charge you an extra fee of 1500 dollars."

At this time I could care less about what price they throw out to get this information on her.

"That's fine," I reply, "just shoot with the info."

"Okay," clearing his throat, "when our system found that Miss Turner had a loan out on her house. We went in a little deeper to see what she spent it on, right? To see why she is in that kind of debt."

"Okay."

"So in most cases when someone with a degree in her field is in debt we automatically assume they took a loan out to pay off student loans, failed to pay it back or put it up for a bond... let me see here."

I hear his fingers tapping down on the keyboard. If this niggah don't get on with what I need to move on with my life. It seems like every time you have to use somebody they take their sweet ass time to do what they need to do for you. On the other hand, I've been fucking with this backend dark web tech company for years. They stay off the grid, so I don't ever have to worry about getting jammed up with their ass.

Clacking on the mouse a few more times.

"Oh there it is!" His sharp voice blurts out, "so we found out that she had over 500,000 dollars in casino fees that she owed but when we hacked into the casino's system the debt had been cleared up in that same week."

"Well, I mean she is one of the highest paid prosecutors in the city, I'm sure she has the money. What could be the reason why she's in debt?"

"Well," he replies, "when the paper trail ended with her debt magically disappearing we discovered something that may peak your interest."

I'm sure nothing is going to blow my mind these days. I just want this information to use it against her to get this shit over with. I can picture her lips dropping lower than they did a few weeks ago when I fuck over her reputation.

"I saw she has a close associate with the name, Bobby Jeffery, correct?"

"Her assistant." I reply.

"Yes, it appears that Mr. Jeffery has three older step brothers and a silent partner who owns the Night Town Casino."

I prepare myself for what he's about to say but I already have a slight idea of what it is. Then I get to thinking and putting two and two together.

I cut in, "his brothers are holding the debt over her head in order for his dumb ass to be on her side, aren't they?"

"Well, it looks like after his mother passed his brothers cut him off from the family fortune, freezing him out of joint bank accounts, the whole nine, for reasons we don't have. Being that the order was to get information on Miss Turner."

"Yes, yes." I say.

This shit is wild. I knew for weeks that something wasn't right about Keisha having one of the most unaware door knobs at her side as counsel. Now I see that both of their asses are broke on the low. I'm more than confused. If his family cut him off, and they're not the ones making her fuck with him, what is it? He probably blackmailing the shit out of her...or they doing drugs together for all I know. He always says the most off the wall shit to the same judges that can bury his ass in contempt, but I mean what else can you expect from a niggah with two first names.

He goes on to say, "from what we picked up in the system Mr. Jeffery's ex-husband is indeed the silent partner of the Night Town Casino... we discovered that when the divorce was finalized Mr. Jeffery won the rights to half of Mr. Crown's family fortune, including proceeds from the Night Town Casino."

What the fuck?! That explains it all! Cold world out here. Adding to Bobby being the luckiest son of a bitch in the world. He is smarter than I thought. Had to be. No telling what he did to get into it with all his people. They are his step brothers though. It's rare to be extra close to those muthafuckas unless you grew up with each other from childhood. Fuck it. I have more work than ever to do to get all these fuckers caught up in my web. I feel more than refreshed too. Ball's in my court now bitches!

"Wow, so Bobby is still loaded with cash," I reply, "Thank you for your time."

"Oh sure no problem at all, please let us know if you need anything else."

"Sure thing, I will have the payment wired to your account. Same one under Crowdfund Investments BTC, right?"

"Yup! That's it."

Catching him before he hangs up, "hey as a matter of fact I do have another job for you." I say.

"Yes, what can I do for you?"

"I need you to do a search for a guy with the name Roshaun Cole."

"Sure thing Mr. Staxx."

I hang up the phone to a mind full of ideas. That's what I love about my white folks in the D. They're going to get what I need without any questions asked, right down to business. I can expect to hear from them in a few weeks, if not in a couple of days. If my girl Sam gets back in the office, I'll have my info in no time.

Reversing it back to all the fools around me, they're in a handful of shit. Starting with Tristian's young ass thinking he can play me for a dummy. He could have assumed that if he gave me a bone I would bite. With everything going on in my life I don't blame him. Still, he better have one solid ass reason for betraying my trust before his ass is on the street looking for another gig.

Calling out my office's door, "Tristian, come here please." I say.

The oldest trick in the book is to get the guard down before going in for the kill. If I show him that I'm concerned about his wellbeing, he's going to tell me everything that I need to know. A soft boy like Tristain can't handle that kind of pressure, also letting me know he will always tell the truth when his back is up against the wall.

Chapter 11

Diamond In The Ruff

We don't discriminate at Clutch Case Law Firm. That's why the reason to believe he's been creeping around with Bobby can be why he had that little information on Keisha in the first place. I wouldn't put it past Bobby's old ass to play with a young boy's head to get what he wants. It's obvious he saw an opportunity to learn my system and why not do that by tricking my brand new assistant to get the juice.

He pokes his head through the door, "yes Sir?" He asks.

"Come have a seat and shut the door behind you."

Closing it behind his back he takes a seat across from my desk, crossing his legs over each other.

"Hey so I called you in because I wanted to thank you for all the great work you've been doing, especially since I've been out for a few days."

His face lights all the way the fuck up. *Got him.* I understand the respect Tristian has for me, but at the same time he's going to have to learn the real game. That's standing your ground no matter who you're in the face of. Eating up every word a muthafucka got to say is the essence of sacrifice. No one is going to respect you if you stand for nothing. His first lesson starts today.

"Thanks so much Sir! I..."

Waving him to silence, "but let's get straight to it." My voice gets low, "I know you've been lying to me about getting the information from my people and I want to know why?"

His cheeks automatically go from light to red circles. I expect him to hold onto the lie for as long as he can. Both of us are rational enough to hash it out. Even though I may still get rid of that ass after, I think no less of him being a good kid in a fucked up situation.

"I'm sorry Sir but I had to, or he was going to expose me."

"Who is going to expose you?" I ask.

That was easy. Once he tells me he's banging Bobby, telling him my business and shit, he's out the door. It's obvious that he got his information from him. Unless he's seeing Keisha's skank ass too, I wouldn't put it past her to seduce a child for information either.

With his head almost in his lap, "the year in high school. I never really liked to look at boys, but it was this one tall guy who stole my heart," he sighs, "and the more I tried to fight the feelings the more they wouldn't go away and the more I was in danger."

"In danger?" I ask, "in danger from who? I don't understand what you are implying kid?"

Aww shit. He's one of those sympathizing liars. He wants to get my guard down low enough to try to keep his job. One thing these folks are going to have to learn about me is I'm not the Mr. Nice Guy they think I am. When it comes to my business I will eat yo' ass up then spit you the fuck out on the floor.

"My father!" He blurts out, "he's the reason I overdosed in college, and he's the reason I can't stand the touch of a woman because I'd rather have a man's hand rubbing on my skin."

My lips twist around in a few circles. What the hell does this have to do with him having access to the information from screwing Bobby? I am more than remorseful to hear about his sick ass daddy for doing that hoe shit to him, but this is not giving me the answers I need to put Keisha on her ass.

I start to talk, "hey, I'm very sorry about the things your father has done to you," staring into his eyes, "is this why you are sleeping with Bobby?"

"What?!" Sucking his teeth, "Bobby? I would never."

I'm starting to lose all the patience I have left with this guy! His ass better get to talking rather than beating around the bush and quick! He has five seconds before my knuckles go upside his temple.

Sitting up in my chair I lean in on him, "look you need to tell me what's going on," I low key snap, "because if you don't I'm going to assume that you are playing both sides because you fucking around with that prick Bobby."

Looking up he throws his back against the chair.

"Back in 2007 my mom and dad got divorced because my mother was okay that I was gay, but my father played like I wasn't."

"Okay?" I sigh harder.

"Well, my mother never knew that the real reason my father was mad that I had a boyfriend in college is because he was very upset that it wasn't him anymore," remaining still in the chair, "it wasn't until he was fighting a secret divorce with his lover Bobby Jeffery for 30 million dollars and part ownership in his casino called nigh..."

"Night Town Casino..." I finish his words for him.

So it all fits in like the perfect puzzle piece. Tristian's weird ass daddy fucking on Mr. Bobby who is a shitty lawyer by the way, who is also the silent partner of the casino. I mean, who else can it be? He's not screwing one of his brothers I would hope.

"Wow," puffing the air, "I'm very sorry to hear this," I pause, "I just have one question... Why are you in danger because of your father?"

I'll never be able to grasp the amount of pain Tristian experienced from his father. I can only empathize his circumstances, also respecting his courage to go on with his life. I do not care one bit about who he prefers to sleep with, I just need to understand what his dad has over his head to at least help him. With all the shit he has to deal with it'll be downright cold to take away the beginning of his career over a few rookie mistakes. Besides, the way he came up I applaud him for still standing tall.

"Uh-uhm," patting his throat, "I am a bit embarrassed to share so much into my personal life, Sir." He comments.

"Hey," I say, "believe me when I say whatever you say to me will always remain between us."

Swallowing back to back his Adam's apple jumps with his words, "well to be all the way honest with you Sir, there's more. I am so very sorry, and I didn't know you were associated with this person before," he says.

Without thinking my head jumps back, "wha-what? Who are you referring to?"

Lord knows I cannot take any more surprises. The last thing I need is for him to be connected to anyone from my past. Picking my whole brain not a single name comes to mind that he can possibly be talking about. Not one person from my past has knowledge of any of my business associates, I made sure of it a long time ago.

"I met him a few months back and he's the one who pushed me to apply for your front desk, well that's before we broke up.

But being that you have no pictures of you on your website I kind of believed him when he said some crazy things about you."

"Who boy?!" I respond, "who have you been talking to?"

"His name is... his name is Drew Pattenfield he says he grew up with you in a city called Toledo, somewhere in Ohio."

Every single vein in my forehead's ready to pop out and choke this little niggah out until he drops. There's no way this man inserted himself in my life in every way fucking possible. In addition to doing that, he sends another man to get into my business. *Hell no!* Somebody has to die to fucking day! Whether it be Drew or Tristian these niggahs really got me fucked up.

Fighting off the urge to take this little niggah head off I think of a few ways to use him to my advantage. If Tristian is telling the truth which there is a strong possibility that he is, I can work with it.

Knock. Knock.

I guess it's his lucky day.

"Come back later," I shout at the door.

"Oh sorry Sir," the front receptionist says, "but your girlfriend is here to see you."

Oh shit! It's everyone's lucky day around this muthafucka. My baby here to see me....

Almost jumping out my skin, "come in." I say.

The door opens to the most beautiful woman to walk the earth.

"Hey honey," her sweet voice says, "are you ready for that date?"

I would have waited a thousand years for this. The entire room disappears the second my eyes get a hold of Radiance. She stands there in black heels while her hair drapes over her skin tight red dress. I'm 100 percent certain that she doesn't have any makeup on. She doesn't even have to wear any. Even if she did, she would still be immaculate beyond measure.

"Oh! Yes! Yes! My girlfriend," nodding at Linda, "thank you... I look down at Tristain, "hey kid you're free to go."

"But- I... are we good Sir."

Sliding from behind my desk, "yes," keeping my eyes on Radiance, "now get out of here before I change my mind."

Both my assistant and Tristian shoot out of my office.

Smiling from cheek to cheek she asks, "are you okay baby? You look a little upset."

Leading her to the front door, "yes," I smile back, "I am more than okay now."

Although half of the office has their noses in our business I don't give a damn. If I saw a fly ass niggah with a goddess on his arm, I would be staring too. There's nothing in this world that can get in the way of this feeling.

I tell Linda to clear my schedule for today.

Radiance and I head to the place I prepared for her to see days ago. I have many questions about how she spent the days we weren't by each other's side, but that can wait, my stomach bubbles from the fear of the place I'm taking her to not be good enough. I sit next to her in the car with my mind racing about what her reaction is going to look like.

"So, how has life been?" I ask.

With her head facing the window, "it's been good." she replies.

"Oh," nodding my head, "what about the shop? Is it coming along alright?"

"Yup, coming out pretty good as well."

Man what the hell is going through this woman's head? It's been years since we spent any real time together now it's like she's not even into a niggah no more. Maybe I'm reading too deep into it. Or she might have a lot on her mind too. I'm just gone chill until we get there.

After 20 minutes of silence my driver pulls into the parking lot of our destination.

"We're here," I say, "close your eyes."

She closes her eyes as I help her out of the car. Going first, I open the side door of an apartment complex. The building is 12 stories high meaning my fingers are going to be cramping from holding them over on her eyes. We get onto the elevator.

"Devine?" She asks, "should I be scared?"

"What? Baby no, why would you ask that?"

Shaking her leg, "well because, I feel like we've been on an elevator for almost 2 minutes, and I can't see anything."

"Aww baby hush," I laugh, "we're almost there."

When we hit the top floor of the building, I guide her past two men waiting by the door.

Giving them a nod, "keep walking," I say to her.

I take her to the place I go when I need peace of mind. It is like seeing the world for what it really is up there. You get a full view of the bright lights shining. Hundreds of cars riding in and out of the city. The best part about it is the silence. The simple comfort you get when you're up here alone feels like you have the world in your hands instead of on your back.

Sitting at the edge is a table with a dozen of firm red roses, a fresh bottle of Rosay wine and two plates for the dinner the private chef is preparing for us tonight.

Her little voice squeaks, "come on Devine! I want to see."

"You do huh?"

"Ugh! I'm going to bite you...come on please."

Counting down from three I drop both my hands down to my side.

"Wow! This is amazing!"

The look on her face damn near lit up sparks inside my soul.

"You like it?"

"Yes! Where are we?"

"We're at one of my apartment buildings."

"You own this?" She asks. "Wow Devine that is amazing."

Gripping onto her hand I pull the chair back then push her up to the table.

"Aww for me?" She presses her nose into the roses.

"Yes baby," I say, "all for you."

"Aww! You are so sweet Devine... I love it."

At that moment all my problems fade away. Nothing is better than putting a smile on a gorgeous face like Radiance's. You can live a million lives with a woman as brilliant. The world is hers; my world is hers. And I plan to give her everything she's ever wanted.

"How did you get all this together that fast?" She asks.

"Let's just say I get what I need when I need it."

"Mhm," she says with a little smirk."

We sit there, talking, laughing, reminiscing about old times for hours.

"Mhm, so you remember the time when we went to see that new Halloween movie..." "Yeah, Michael Myers," I chip in.

Rolling her eyes, "huh, why do black people always make up their own names for something," she teases, "anyways and you remember when the old man who was always trying to stop him."

"Yeah I think that was his therapist... uhm, I think dude name was Loomis or something like that."

"Yeah! Yeah! Loomis, so why am I in Ohio getting my nails done at the salon and the old Chinese dude doing my nails looks just like him."

"Cap."

She cracks up laughing.

"No for real! And the first thing I do is think back to that night because it was the first time you told me you loved me."

Damn. She got a niggah smiling from ear to ear.

Shit just got real. I don't think this woman realizes how much that love never faded away. I'm starting to believe the only other woman I ever felt like this for before was a childhood crush. Words cannot explain the kind of love I want to have with Radiance. The commitment I want to hold myself up to. Wiping her sweet tears away whenever life gets tough. She's the light that sparks up a light in my world whenever she's around. The thought of her makes my life easier even while everything else is burning down around me.

After dessert we focus on each other.

"How about we take this party back to your place?" She suggests.

Leaning against the table my cheeks stretch out from ear to ear.

"Yes..." I say. "We can definitely do that."

Waving for the men to come clean the table off I grab her hand and escort her back onto the elevator.

Gazing into each other's eyes, it gets harder to fight back the urge of throwing this woman over my shoulder. The shit is driving me full blown crazy.

"This night was amazing," she says, "I never want it to en..."

Fuck it!

Stopping her in her tracks I go in for the kill. Taking hold of her body I throw her back up against the elevator wall. Squeezing a handful of her left ass cheek in my right hand our lips clash.

Life doesn't even know how long I needed this girl in it. How long I waited for her to fall out of the sky. I can't wait to get back to my house to show her either.

She takes the fingers on my left hand and shoves them up her dress. Caressing her clit with my fingertips my mind goes blank. *Damn!* This shit so tight.

Snatching my dick in her hands, her breath blows across my neck.

"Uh! Yes daddy," she whispers loudly.

The second the elevator hits the ground floor I jump back when the ding sounds off.

She paints in the air. "Why'd you stop?!"

Tugging on the collar of my suit I face forward, "because my driver is waiting on the other side of that door," I reply.

"So?!"

Taking her hand, "so wouldn't want to take his eyes out from seeing my Queen exposed," I toss out a slick grin.

Twisting her eyes, "oh shush," shoving my arm, "he knows this pussy is only to be witnessed for your eyes."

"He better know."

My driver greets us at the car, "where to Sir?" He asks, "taking Miss Strodem home."

"Yes," I reply, "take 'us' home."

I can't help myself around this woman. It's taking any amount of strength I have to not lay her down on this back seat. Instead, I find myself with a soft grip on her thigh until we reach my front porch.

She gapes at the few cars in my driveway, and her eyes shift up to my patio under my roof. "Wow, you have a beautiful home," she says.

Opening the door, "thank you," I'm smiling inside, "I can give you a quick tour of the house."

"Or a quick tour of the bedroom."

Without warning she slams the door with her back, pushing me a few steps backwards. She first snatches my jacket off, my shirt, last my pants. She got me standing in my living room butt ass naked. Next thing I know we in my bedroom not letting each other get a speck of air to breathe.

I'm loving every bit of this shit. Her fine ass got my dick more solid than it's ever been before.

"Yes baby!" She moans out.

Laying on top of her my lips starts from her belly button straight to her pussy. The second I rub my lips across her smooth and tender lips. I stick my tongue straight into her hole. *Oh my God!* Everything about this girl is gorgeous down from the taste of her juices.

"Mhm," in a few grunts, "this shit so good."

The blood in my chest is pumping my heart up 50 times over. After flipping her on her stomach I smack her ass, stuffing my whole face in between her cheeks, I make a mess.

"Ouu! Daddy," she screams, "please... I need you inside me."

My head all fucked up I come up for air again...

"Tell me you want it." I say.

"I want it! Uhh! I want it please!"

Holding my dick with one hand I pull her up, pushing down on her back to give me that arch like she used to.

Blowing out some air, "huh!" She moans.

It's so warm, and tight that you can take a nap in this shit. Aww man, where did this woman come from? I stroke so deep in her that it feels like I got lost in a deep abyss with no way out.

"Turn around," I flip her on her back.

She wraps her arms and legs around me so tight that I barely have room to move. My body can only twist around in small circles. So I get to deep stroking her shit until I have all her insides on this dick.

A few tears dropping down her face, "I missed you so much baby," she says.

Groaning back, "ouu, baby I missed you too," I huff, "I want you in my life forever..."

"Me too baby."

I keep stroking, "I love you so much," I groan again.

Both her hands grip my face, "I love you too Devine," pressing her lips to mine.

I slow up just a little bit to keep me from busting a nut too early. I look down to make sure she gets hers first. And oh man, my dick has more cream on it than a cone. *I'm about to kill this lil shit.* At a careful speed I pump faster and faster.

"Yes! Harder daddy!"

The quicker I go the tighter her hole gets around my dick and the louder the sounds from her ass clapping on my thighs turns me on more.

"Shit!" I yell out.

I swear a brain vessel busted inside my temple at the same time.

Our bodies fell into the bed.

"Oh wow," she pants, "I guess sex gets better with age too."

Chapter 12

Nite And Day

Laughing, I get up to go get her a warm towel out of the bathroom. All I can assume is she had a great time. A part of me don't want the night to end at all. I wish we can sit in my room together forever. Making new memories for each other to think about every day.

"Here you go baby."

She's still in the same spot I left her. *I laid her fine ass out.* Wiping our juices off of her coochie I notice a small line, almost faded going across the top of it. *What the hell?* From my experience when you see scars it's from surviving a fight or shootout in the hood. Now days you have all these BBL's and shit.

"What happened here sweetheart?" I ask.

Sitting up she snatches the towel then puts her legs together.

"It-it's nothing," she sighs.

I jump onto the bed, "it's okay baby... you can always talk to me." I cuddle her arm.

For a second she stares into space. Figuring she's gathering her thoughts I wait patiently for her to speak.

"Well, you know I left the city to be with my sister in her time of need."

"Yeah," I reply, "how is she doing by the way."

Immediate tears begin to drop into her lap.

"Sh-she's dead."

What the fuck?! This is an extreme turn of events. I didn't have a single clue that her big sister passed away. Knowing how close they were that shit puts a hold on my soul.

"Aww baby I'm so sorry," squeezing her into my arms, "what happened? If you don't mind me asking of course."

Pulling back she wipes the remaining tears from her eyes, "I don't know much," sniffling, "all I know is her boyfriend got mixed up with the wrong people, and they went after her. I tried everything I could to save her."

"Who did he get mixed up with?" I ask.

"I don't know," her voice cracks, "All I know is one day we woke up blindfolded the next day they both were gone an-and... I don't want to talk about it anymore please."

Damn. I never want to see my baby hurt like this. I can't take the pain away from her heart, but I can find whoever did this to her. And when I do I'm going to fuck every single last one of these muthafuckas world's up. Nobody is ever going to get over on mine!

We both get silent.

She lays back down on the bed, "you know after I left there wasn't a day that passed by without me thinking about you."

I lay next to her, "same here baby, after you left... the pain was... that pain was, unexplainable."

Pulling the cover over her legs I kiss her forehead.

"Devine," she says, "you know when I left I had no choice but to, right?"

"Yeah baby, I understand. I would have left for one of my brothers too."

"Are you guys seeing eye to eye now?"

Pulling her into my chest, "pshh, you know how that shit go... you give a muthafucka an inch they take a mile," I reply, "besides I'm so busy with this case I can't pull myself to focus on anymore family drama."

Even though I don't fuck with any of my brothers I would never want to see them gone. We didn't really grow up together after my mom left my dad. I helped raise my little cousins at Ma house instead. With everyone from home either thinking I'm dead or just don't give a fuck, I made my mind up that it'll be easier to keep it that way.

I also love how she remembers the things I told her years ago. It makes me feel good to have a ride or die on my side. Someone who I can trust is better than being a mouse in a pit of snakes. My luck is getting better by the day.

"Go to sleep baby," I say, "I got you."

I doze off as soon as I rock her to sleep.

The next morning I wake up to a whiff of cinnamon going across my nose. Peeping out the corner of my eye at the clock, it's almost time for me to get to the office.

"Good morning honey bun."

Radiance brings me a plate with eggs, turkey bacon on top of French toast.

Grabbing the plate, "thank you baby," I say, "this looks delicious."

I can never forget her skills in the kitchen. My girl throws it down up in that thang you hear me.

After I get done with my food she takes the plate back to the kitchen.

"Hey baby," she calls out, "don't you have to go to work today?"

Looking back to the clock it's half past eight thirty.

"No," I reply, "I took a few da... weeks off."

The idea just hit me that being the boss makes it possible for me to do whatever the fuck I want. No one can question me about it either. I know Tristian's probably on edge worrying about if he's going to lose his job, but I'll deal with that when the time comes. I might let him keep it to leave my hands extra clean when that bum Drew comes up missing.

In other words I'm not allowing anything to get in the way of my baby's time right now. I promised myself if she ever came back in my life I was going to give her everything under the sun.

That starts today.

"Hey baby, come here." I say.

Rolling over to the edge of the bed I lay my head in her lap as she sits on the bed.

"Yes honey," she says, "how did you sleep?"

"Peachy," I smirk, "I have a surprise for you though."

She smiles, "and what's that?"

"Well if I told you it wouldn't be a surprise now would it?"

Arching both her eyebrows at me, "okay well I have to go get some clothes from the..."

"I know what you like, I'll take care of that."

"Okay, well at least let me wash the rest of the dishes."

"Uhn Uhn," I grab her waist, "let me take care of you."

Smashing my head in between her legs I force my tongue on her clit. Circling it around in slow circles I feel her legs buck. *Ouu!* I like that. You know when a woman's trying her hardest to hold on to her orgasm, knowing she's about to blow. So I go faster.

Twirling the tip of my tongue in circles I take a peek at her eyes rolling to the back of her head.

Stabbing her nails into the back of my head.

"Oh my go-gosh!" She screams.

Her back slams onto the bed at the same time that all her juice squirts onto my tongue.

I swallow all of them. "Mhm, you still taste good." I laugh.

She's laid out in the bed like a crash dummy.

"I-I can't move."

I jump up and head to the shower.

"You'll be just fine."

After my driver pulls up with her clothes we head out to one of my favorite spots in the city, Griffith Park. Man, we're having the time of our lives here. We've already been on the Ferris wheel, saw the lions, not to mention me damn near losing my life fucking with one of the bobcats running around this muthafucka. I haven't enjoyed myself like this in forever.

Standing under the Hollywood sign I squeeze her tighter then peck her on the forehead.

"Aww baby," she jumps into my arms, "this was one of the best days of my life."

"I'm glad you had a good time baby." I say.

My eyes hit the ground with the rest of my face when a quick thought about my current life resurfaces.

"What's wrong?"

"It's just... I'm going through so much in my work life right now and after the time I have off I don't think it's going to get any better."

"Anything you care to talk about?" She asks.

"Can't get too personal," I reply, "just know I have to be extremely careful with my next moves. They actually have to be my best moves."

"Well, you know what I think?" She asks, "I you think that you are one of the strongest men I've ever met, and you can get through anything."

That's what I like most about Radiance. She always finds a way to remain positive in a negative situation. The other thing I loved most is she doesn't ever force me to go deep into my problems unless I give her the green light too. I remember sharing some of my deepest secrets with her back then. She is and always will be the one person I trust most in the world.

My eyes gazing into hers our lips embrace. "I love you." I say.

Batting her eyes I can feel her heart racing a thousand miles a minute.

"I love you too Devine."

The way her voice vibrates through my ears sends fireworks to light up my universe. I don't have to look any further. The woman of my dreams dropped right back in my lap no question. I'm in love. And moving too fast isn't quick enough for what she deserves. From this day forward I swear to protect, serve, and honor her in addition to knocking her light bulbs loose anytime she wants me to.

"Come back to my house tonight?" I ask.

Mindful of her answer already I lead her to the car. On the way home I can't wait to lay next to her tonight. Just the tone of her soft skin makes my dick hard as fuck. And by the way she keeps biting her bottom lip. She makes it obvious she wants me just the same. This will never get old.

"Baby?"

"Yes my love," she replies.

"I want you to leave a few of your things at my house."

"Oh... uhm."

I cut in, "and I know it's fast but it's just something in me that tells me you're the one... matter of fact I knew you were six years ago and..."

"Yes," cutting me off, "I would love to."

Swallowing hella hard, "for real?"

She smirks back, "Devine, back then I knew you were the one too and sometimes I think about if I stayed with you what my life would be like."

Tightening the grip on her hand, "baby, you don't have to worry about anything else." I say, "I am going to take care of you forever."

I kiss her forehead.

After a few minutes she knocks out on my lap before we make it back to the house.

My driver opens the door, "need help Sir?" He asks.

"Yeah, here are the keys, go open my front door for me."

Lifting her up in my arms I take her in the house then lay her out on the bed. I wave him off and head into the living room after I take her clothes off.

My baby's knocked out. I smile to myself. To my surprise I'm not that tired. I actually have so much on my mind that I can't think straight. Taking my phone out of my pocket I cut it on at the same time as turning on the TV.

Ding. Ding. Ding. Ding. Ding.

Damn. Back to the messy part of my life. I unlock the screen to almost eighty messages from everyone who knows me. The first three messages are from Keisha's mad ass threatening my whole life, Tristian begging for a job he didn't even lose yet, I keep scrolling past the few messages from one of Javeon's watch dogs ordering information. And stop at an unknown number which is

141

most likely Lethal with 'no leads on the fish's location'. *Huh!* Sometimes I want to throw this muthafucka in the garbage.

Time will only tell if my life is going to change for the better. With Radiance on my side I know for sure that it has to.

The next couple of hours with Radiance turn into days. It feels like time is flying, next thing I know we're into the last few weeks of this case. I've been enjoying every second, day, and night of what she's doing to me. Making my days in court fly by, the evenings in the office brighter. I can't begin to count the number of places where I broke her back. The Santa Monica Pier, Venice Beach, even at Sunset Boulevard.

I'm in the office reminiscing on how my last few months have been a ball. And when this case is over for good I plan to go ghost with my baby. I haven't asked yet, but I already know what her answer will be.

On the other hand Javeon hasn't had the best attitude with the trial, he isn't aware of the plan I have to make Keisha's ass eat dirt. I have the upper hand. It only looks like we're losing the case. When the jury hears the argument I've been putting together, he's going to learn how to shut the fuck up for once. Everything's going the way I need it to go.

Knock! Knock!

"Mr. Staxx?"

With a huge smile I say, "aww my baby came right on tim..."

A flash of lightning bolts through my chest.

"You bastard!"

What the fuck?!

All I see is a big ass head busting through my office door like the raid squad.

"Sir I'm sorry but Miss Turner demanded to..."

Busting in the door past Linda, "Bitch shoo!" Keisha yells.

"Aye!" I shout out, "you need to chill out."

I stay seated to let her make a fool of herself.

"Linda," looking over Keisha's shoulder I say, "everything is okay, just shut the door behind you please."

Linda closes the door.

I'm not surprised by her visit at all. I'm fully aware of her reason for popping up to my shit. As a matter of fact her showing up here was expected.

Slamming a tan folder on my desk. "You filed a motion to dismiss the case," she says, "on what grounds of your fucked up audacity do you think you have a chance to get my case canned?!"

The shaking in her voice tells me the whole lot of what she's really thinking. Her mindset isn't where it needs to be at all. Especially not in my office checking my temperature. Sadly for her that is right where I need it to be.

"Listen," crossing my arms, "first of all the facts you have in this case are shitty." "Excuse me?!" She shouts.

"Why don't you lower your voice and have a seat."

I imagined the shit look on her face a little different. The bitch is paying regardless though just off the death threats she's been sending me after court for the last few months alone. How mad can a broad be for not getting any play from a niggah. Then again, I am that niggah. I'd be mad too if I was her.

I smirk as she flops down on the chair, "exhibit A," taking out a piece of paper, "you see I've been taking a look at your bullshit motion of discovery, and I noticed you have a lot of empty leads that cannot on any ground accuse my client specifically for being the Kingpin of Hotboyz Corporation."

Throwing the paper on the desk it shows a witness statement from one of the niggahs I used to run with in the streets. A few months ago he had an accident, which we all know what really happened to bruh, and nobody has heard from him since.

Twisting her eyes, "and my other four witnesses," tossing the paper back at me, "who magically had a heart attack, fell in front of a car, or went missing over the years," she says, "but we all know what happened to them."

"You have a point, their accidents are very unfortunate which makes it inadmissible in court though," throwing out another piece of paper, "exhibit B, which states that my client has a treacherous reputation in the streets which indeed also does not matter in the courtroom, in fact it is hearsay which is not admissible in evidence unless it is specifically allowed by an exception to the rules of evidence or another statute," uncrossing my arms, "and seeing that your fifth witness, Drew Stantenfield who made this statement is indeed not in your protection anymore he will not be testifying in your argument on the stand."

The bubbles in her eyes are priceless. This proves again that I'm not the niggah to be fucked with. But I have a heart, I'll give her one more chance to back down before I really go in on her ass. I enjoyed all the months where she thought she did her big one. There is no match for me in this law shit. I am the definition of a trapper turned public figure. At least in the state of California.

She says, "oh you think you know something because my C.I. ditched us?" She asks, "and I bet you told your client, huh?"

"Oh Keish, you know I'd never break the law."

"Mhm," she smiles, "don't be fooled my baby. I have one more eyewitness who is going to tear both you and that slow-ass criminal of yours a new asshole," raising to her feet, "and when I'm done with you, your reputation is going to be that favorite word you like to use, trash."

I'm more than aware of her client Roshaun. I know she's more mad that she can't get any real evidence to prove Javeon's dangerous enough to fund his witness protection. I really wish my white girl would get back in the office to handle what needs to be done. It don't matter, that little dude will be taken care of as soon as they get back to me with his location. Little does she know nobody is going to fuck up what I got going on. This case is sealed air tight in my favor, might as well wrap it up with a bow right now.

I hold in my laughs long enough to let her feel like she's doing something. This hoe is the smartest, dummy I've ever met. On the other side of all of this she feels that sting of defeat in her chest. I am the man, and she knows it. Everyone knows it. Hell, her mammy knows it.

"Cut the shit." I say, "you're going to back down and dismiss the case."

Digging her nails into my desk, "or what?" she asks, "or you're going to make a fool out of yourself once I hang your ass?"

I rise to her level, "or someone is going to accidentally expose Keisha Turner for being in debt from that gambling problem she has," I reply.

"Bull shit," she says, "you can't prove anything of that nature."

"Oh really? You know what? You may be right but one thing I can prove is the fact that your little... I mean, big partner over there is holding that same casino debt that his ex-husband has over your head."

There it is! The face drop I've been waiting to see for what seems like forever. *Checkmate.* No way she'll ever put her entire life at risk. Not even to win a case over. This is where she better throw in the towel rather than pissing my soul off more than she already has.

Backing up towards the door, "oh," nodding her head, "so this is how it's going to be huh?"

Dropping back to my chair, "don't test me."

We stare in silence.

"Alright," she says, "I'll have my people look over the details and drop the RICO charge... but with the severity of the case between your client and a comatose Fed he is still looking at least 10 years."

I reply, "which can't be proved that my client had any hand in that, inadmissible, make it 5 and I'll tell my people over at the newspaper that I don't have the story for the article after all. "

With a soft smirk, "you son of a bitch," she says, "now I see how you win all your cases."

Knock. Knock.

"Mr. Staxx," Linda says, "your girlfriend is here to see you."

Shit! I forgot all about Radiance coming for lunch this afternoon. There is no way Keisha is going to stay cool when she sees how fine my babe is. She's going to find out fast that my baby isn't for the bullshit either though. I hope this bitch don't say some slick shit that makes me show my true colors at my place of work.

"Tell her I'll be out in a sec."

"Oh no," Keisha smiles, "he'll be out right now."

Opening the door to Radiance standing next to Linda. *Damn she fine!* The first thing that comes to mind, the second is me keeping my composure from knocking this thot upside that wig.

"Hey baby!" Radiance smiles.

"Mhm," Keisha stares into her eyes, "so this is the bop's jacket I found at your place a few weeks back?"

"Excuse me?" Radiance replies.

"Uhm-uhm," I say, "Linda please escort Miss Turner to the front door."

If I act out, Radiance is going to worry. Man it's taking everything in me to keep my cool.

Snatching her arm away from Linda, "uhn-uhn! Don't touch me," she yells, "let me tell you something girl you're going to end up just like his dead assistant they're about to bury in the ground," she looks at me, "oh yeah! And I heard you was fucking her too!"

"More hearsay," I call out at the door, "Security! Please get Miss Turner out of my office."

Chapter 13

Ain't No Love In The Streets

Security rushes to grab Keisha's mickied ass up to put her back where she belongs.

Her voice echoes. "Everyone he gets close to never survives! He is the real menace to society!" She yells out.

I hurry to Radiance's side. "Baby, I'm so sorry about that."

"Who was that?" She asks.

Guiding her to the chair my mind starts racing around in circles. How are they about to bury Alesha in the ground? If they found her body I didn't hear anything about it. This isn't making any sense.

I grab my phone to send Tristian an immediate text, *send Alesha's funeral details, location, whatever asap.*

"Is everything okay?" Radiance asks.

My response can't be too specific right now, I got a lot of explaining to do, but not at this moment.

My head down in my phone, "yes, yes." I reply, "that was the nut case Keisha I was telling you about."

"Ooh the Prosecutor on your recent case."

"Yes," I say.

Ding. My phone buzzes with a message from Tristian. *Cedar Hill Mortuary & Accommodation, 1722 Colorado Blvd. Los Angeles, California 90041.*

Popping up out of the chair I head for the door.

"Baby," I say, "I'm so sorry, but I have something so important I have to do, and it can't wait."

"But, okay... wait honey slow down," she utters, "is this about that lawyer lady? I'm not understanding."

She walks with me out of the door as I signal Tristian to order my driver to the front of the building.

"Listen Babe I'm so sorry, but I'm going to meet you at my house later, okay?!" I peck her on the cheek then hop inside the car.

Fuck! The only thing going through my head is the amount of agony I'm about to face if somebody found this girl's body. If anything the police would have been picked me up if they found it. Another thing is if I know anything it's that Lethal's killer instincts are rarely wrong and having burial sites where no one looks is one of them.

Regardless of the heavy traffic it takes nothing but twenty minutes to make it to the funeral home. I get out of the car, seeing a few people standing in front of the building I tug on the collar of my suit.

"Hey, you don't have to wait," I say to my driver, "I may be here for a while."

"Yes, Sir." He replies.

Assuming it's been going on for at least a few hours I hold my breath until I get inside the doors. *Get in, scope some shit out, say some prayers, get out.* I say to myself. Walking past a few people sitting on the benches I ignore the few eyes glued on my presence. I make it to the front of a closed casket. I don't have a clue right now. Either I'm late as hell or she's not in this muthafucka. Either way, the choir is still singing, the seats are full of people, and a woman who's rocking back and forth is coddling a fist full of tears. Seeing that she looks just like Alesha with her long hair, hanging over her all black one piece I have to get into her mind.

I approach her, "hello," looking into her eyes, "you must be Alesha's mother?" I ask.

Although I'm more than tense about the words that's about to come out of her mouth, a real man has to always stand on his words.

Patting her eyes with a tissue, "Sorry," she sniffles, "Who are you?"

Introducing myself, "I am Devine Staxx," I grab her hand, "I own the law firm over on Atlantic Boulevard."

"Oh," squeezing my hand, "you're that nice man she was always telling me about... her boss right?"

A deep chill courses up my spine.

" Yes ma'am, I heard late a few months ago that she was missing but I'm so very sorry for this outcome."

"Yes," she sighs, "me too. A wild fire my daughter was."

Smiling at her, "yes... yes she was," I say, "even as an assistant she was a force to be reckoned with."

Without going so far into detail I give her my information to extend a hand out for anything she may need. Like her daughter, she's simple to read, still she didn't give me any insights on whether Alesha is in the casket or not. The bright side is that if they did find her no one seems to know who killed her. Which means Lethal knows what he's doing. I still hate that we had to end the way we did though.

Checking out the rest of the venue they put together her decor is pretty nice. I remember her saying her favorite color was purple, so it makes sense that everyone has on purple and black. I make sure to sit in the back so no one recognizes my face.

Ding. Ding. Ding. I peep an unknown number going across my screen back to back. Somebody must have died the way my phone is blowing up. I just hope that it's not Javeon sending more threats to end my career. The more I think about him the more I picture myself hanging him upside down by his feet like he did ol' boy. He makes a niggah want to burn his ass up with his anxious ass. I can't wait to let him in on the deal I made to save him. Everything is finally falling into place.

Heading for the door I feel a hand tap on my shoulder.

"Hey." A soft voice says, "aren't you my sister's boss?"

I turn around to a young girl holding a little boy on her waist.

I reply, "yes I am," holding out my hand, "and you must be Alesha's..."

"Sister," finishing my sentence she says, "I'm her little sister on her dad's side."

"And this must be her son," tugging on the boy's arm, "hey guy."

Damn. I drop my phone to my side. I didn't know Alesha had a little sister. She has to be seventeen no older than eighteen at the most. From her mother, son, to her sister, they all spit images of each other. Another thing I can agree on is the beauty between them all. Her son even has her genes strong.

"Like I told your mother I'm so sorry for your loss and if you ever need anything please be sure to let me know."

"I will," her neck twists, "but I really wanted to let you know I don't appreciate you making my sister cry either." She replies, "she told me all about what y'all had going on."

"Excuse me sweetheart?"

Aww man! This can't be happening right now. What she mean by that? It's always that one person, place or thing to fuck up something when success is almost at the finish line. Is she making a threat? There is no way of being 100 percent sure until I pick her brain. Besides, this little girl has no chance of outsmarting me.

"You ain't gotta play dumb with me Mr. Staxx," she put Alesha's son down, "or Mr. Greyhound whatever your name is."

Stopping the veins from exploding into my forehead I ease in closer to her.

This little girl must not know who she's fucking with, and it shows. If for a second she believes this conversation is going to go any different she is in for a rude awakening. She better quit before she can't.

Ding. Ding. My phone goes off again.

Ignoring the buzz in my hand I attempt to throw her off with a smile.

"I don't have any idea who that is," I say, "you have the wrong person."

She eases closer to me, "oh yeah," she smirks, "a few months ago an ugly dude meets up with my sister wanting info on you, next thing you know my sister's missing. I did some digging in her room and found a whole folder with notes talking about some dude named Jonathan Greyhound. After more digging, found out it's you."

"You can't prove that." I reply.

"Try me. I can show it to my mom, or you can simply give me what I want."

Oh this little bop. I guess the apples don't fall too far from the sibling tree either. It's been months meaning she could have been turned this information into the Feds. As mad as I am, if I can prevent putting another body in the dirt I'll do whatever. In a way

I can respect that she is playing her hand well. Checking my temperature in a room full of Alesha's friends and family is smart. However, she has to be really conniving or really needs something to be able to hold onto her sister's alleged killer.

Peeping out the scene I step back, "what do you want?" I ask.

She says to Alesha's son, "go find grandma," looking back at me, "I want a million." she says, "and I want it by the end of the week."

"A million dollars?!" I burst out.

A few heads in the crowd turn their heads to us. Clearing my throat to throw them off I wave my hand through the air.

"Sorry, something in my throat," I say.

Dun. Dun. Dun. Dun. Dun. Dun. Dun. Someone is blowing my phone backwards.

I turn back to her, "listen…"

"Alex," she adds.

"Alex," I say, "we'll have to finish this conversation later."

"No," she replies, "you're going to meet me beside the Neverland Ranch at the end of this week with my money."

Glancing down at my phone, "alright." I mug her, "but you're going to bring me those files."

I hit her mother with a smug smile while I rush out of the door.

The nerves of this family makes you not give a fuck about them at all. At least her mother has a bit of sense. She will never get a million dollars out of these pockets! I'll give her some money for her loss, I damn sure have to make sure my business don't get in the ears of anyone else that'll force me to cut them muthafuckas off.

Speeding past some more people on the sidewalk.

"Hello?" I answer the phone. "Hello?"

Nothing instead of a rough breath breathing into the phone.

"Hermano," Lethal says, "Brother... we-we caught the fish."

"What?!" My lips smash into the phone. "Where are you?"

This is it! The news I've been gearing up to hear for months.

"Warehouse on the Pine and Main, come quick."

The phone clicks.

Fuck! Of course it has to be right around the corner from Radiance's shop. This niggah has a way of handling his business. For certain I can trust wherever he is the skeletons he catches will never come out the closet. He always has a knack for 'no survivors' to put him in a chokehold of any kind. All I know is the sooner I make it to the warehouse the better.

Bad news on my end is the day I choose to give my driver a break. I need him the most. If anyone on this side of town sees a dude running down the street with thousand dollar Gucci loafers on they're gonna run my pockets. Good thing I didn't always have a driver to run me around.

I cut through one of the short cuts I used to take to meet Radiance a few years back. The huge coincidence is that the alley leads up to the back of her shop. A part of me is worried if I don't make it there fast enough, the number of fingers Lethal's going to cut off that muthafuckas hand...with their history I better put extra speed into my steps.

"Shit," wheezing out for air.

Damn, I done got chubby as fuck. All these months I was up baby girl's ass. I should've gone to the gym at least a few times out of the week. Despite that I'm almost there, creeping past her shop is a huge risk I'd rather die than take. I twist my watch around to look at the time, it's going on eight p.m. I'm sure she's waiting on me at the house by now. I take another peek around the corner to make sure she isn't taking out the trash or anything.

Looking at it I get to thinking about what's taking her so long to open this boy up. If it was up to me, I would've had hell of customers at her front door. I feel bad for not knowing the answer to that question. I been so wrapped up in turning her into my peace that showering her in materialistic shit is all I gave her. After I make it home to my baby tonight I'm going to shower her in all the love and affection that she needs from me. And after I beat this case up tomorrow we taking the first jet somewhere out of the country.

I blow out another breath, preparing to take off past her shop. *One, two ,thr...* What the fuck is this?! I catch a glimpse of Radiance chopping it up with some dark-skinned niggah with locs at her back door. I'm about to blow dude's mouth back. *Calm down bro.* I try to think within reason but all I see is red!

So I get to fighting hard with myself.

If I rush over there without rationally thinking the situation anything can happen. First of all, who is this clown? I start to brainstorm. They not arguing. It might be her brother... nah, he light skin. Or her uncle visiting from Ohio... can't be, she told me he died a few years back... This lady got me fucked all the way up. *Fuck it!* I say to myself. Go all in or go home, right?!

Without taking another peek around the corner I head towards them.

"Ahh!" I shout out, "what the fuck?!"

I hit the ground. A flash of two niggahs in face masks hems me up and throws a bag over my head.

"Get off me!"

This not my first go round of being snatched up. Accepting the fact that I have to die someday it just might be right now. It's been years since a muthafucka played with me like this. I feel like a bitch!

Dragging my legs across the ground I hear some tires screeching then a door slide back before they throw me inside after what sounds like a van skirts off. I remain calm. Tightening some metal around my wrists I figure they're handcuffs when they squeeze them tighter.

"Yeah boss," a hard voice speaks up, "we have the target."

"What?" I ask, "what the fuck y'all want?"

I can't see shit.

A hand pushes a phone up to my ear.

"Yeah, so I see this the only way a niggah can get yo attention."

No fucking way am I at all surprised! This muthafucka Javeon looney ass doing some looney shit is not above him. This man is going to be the death of a niggah alone. Question is, why in the fuck would he have his flunkies pick me up?

Puffing through the bag, "oh hey Javeon," I say, "you sure know how to get it, huh?"

"Fuck all that," he replies, "this is just an alarm clock waking you up for our big day tomorrow and how important it is that yo' ass betta see through on yo' promises."

"Yes, I do... now why don't you have your boys let me go."

Ahh! I got better shit to do than be harassed by a couple of pussy's I can fuck up with this bag on my head. This day has been the most eventful. Even being caught up can't take away the amount of pain I'm going to put in whoever Radiance was talking too. Javeon can do whatever he wants.

His voice echoes in the phone, "mhm, you think it's a game Ace, but I know what a make yo' blood boil," he goes on, "I know how much yo' ass love making it back to that big, nice ass spot you got."

"You won't kill me," smacking my lips, "if you do, who's going to get you out of jail the next time you need to beat a case?"

He laughs, "oh think I won't? That's cute. How bout' I start with that little bitch you been fucking," pausing, "what her name is... Radiance."

I don't say a word.

"What?" He asks, "cat got your tongue... you know what I alway think about? How you used to be the real G of the neighborhood, maybe you could've been better than me at this shit. Now look at you, a bigger pussy than yo' old man."

This little niggah here.

I speak up, "I'll tell ya what, you have ya little guard dogs take me back where the fuck they got me before you be buried under the jail niggah."

"Oh, there he go! Now that's the niggah that taught me everything I know," He laughs, "just one last question, do you think smoking yo' own bitch is what made you into a coochie like yo' pappy?"

"Man fuck you niggah!" I yell out.

Giving him a reaction is the last thing I want to do. This lil' niggah gone make me buss a cap in his skinny ass my damn self. I cannot wait to get rid of this dude once and for all. The minute the judge grants him his sentence I'm moving out of the state. He is a succa ass little boy with power. That is a deadly combination to have in the game. Nothing good ever comes from it.

He can throw shots about my dad all day. I don't give one fuck, the only thing I care about right now is getting the fuck out of this stinking ass van.

One of the dudes takes the phone off of my ear.

"Remember Ace," Javeon's voice sounds over the speaker, "you get me what I want, and all your secrets stay secret...

especially since you seem to kill all your bitches and we wouldn't want to scare off your current hoe, now would we?"

The minute the phone hangs up, my handcuffs are taken off then I hear the door slide open.

"Fuck." I grunt.

My back hits the ground.

The moment I snatch the bag off my head a bunch of voices yell inside of it.

"This the last house bae, I promise."

Trisha and I are sitting in the hottie we jacked from one of the old heads in the projects.

"But Jonathan you said that after we got this car we were going to leave the city for good." She says.

Trisha's fine ass was the real definition of a ride or die. We did everything together. Hit licks, stole from the fiends, and the best part about being with her is all the top she gave me in the whips we stole.

It was slow after I met her in the store that day but the first time we did it, we both knew we were locked forever. I couldn't resist a woman with natural hair, and her tall white chocolate ass had a headful of it.

We sat in the back of one of the biggest Jamaican drug dealers dope house's out of Toledo. The niggah Luki was loaded with hella dope, pills, money, and weed. I just knew when we hit dude for the bag we would be set for life. All we had to do was get through the back door.

Looking over her shoulder, "okay, but I get to choose what to do with the weed this time," she says, "because yo' ass be smokin' it all up."

Replying with a huge smile on my face, "aight bae, but you gotta give me some of that good stuff when we get out of here." I laugh.

She pushed my shoulder, "stop," lowering her voice, "now I'm going to go look and signal you in when the coast is clear."

"No, what if somebody happens to be there?"

"You said yo' people know for a fact that it's empty this weekend right?"

"Yeah," I replied.

Stretching her hand in the backseat, "so it'll be better if you hold this," handing me the strap, "and I go in first just in case I have to act like I got lost."

Although I most definitely didn't agree with her that night, or ever used a gun, most of her plans always worked. She was the one in school, so I found it better to let her do her thang with the plans. Going with the flow gave me the advantage of reaping the benefits she chose to award me with at night.

I take the gun, "here," handing her a flashlight, "take this... don't forget the two, two, three signals." I say.

"Yeah, yeah," she smiles.

Hopping out of the car she blows me a kiss before walking up to the gate surrounding his back yard. She flashes the light two times which tells me that there's no dogs in sight. I sit back in the yard waiting for the light to go off two more times letting me know the coast is clear. My legs began to shake after a minute and a half without the signal. Praying that she don't send me three flashes of light, I get out of the car.

"Trisha," I whisper loudly.

Chapter 14

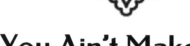

You Ain't Make Me;
You Can't Break Me

"**W**here you at bae?"

After not hearing her voice or anything I creep through the gate to an empty backyard. I still don't see her, but I see the back door cracked open. Gripping tighter on the nine I push the door open with the tip.

I whisper again, "Trisha... where you at girl?"

"Ahh! Stop! Get off of me!"

I went through some double doors that led into what a couple homies said should've been the living room.

"Trisha!" I yelled. "Get the fuck off her!"

My body froze in the threshold. At that point in time I couldn't think of a single thought that could save her from the gang of men surrounding her smushing her frail body into the bed.

Looking around at all her clothes ripped up and spread all over the floor. I damn near lose my mind.

I cock back the trigger.

Hell of blood rushed to my head. The first thing I thought to do was blast all the they ass, the tears gushing out of her eyes making them red as she looked up begging for my help almost took me out by itself. The man laying on top of her pumped in and out smiled at me.

"Fuck!"

The power from the bullet leaving the chamber made the gun drop out my hand.

"What the fuck?!"

They all screamed out. What the fuck did you do?!

Wiping the blood from my forehead I take off out of the door at the sight of Trisha panting out for air.

The rest is a blur from there. The last thing I remember is being in handcuffs with blue lights flashing over my head. That was the first night I saw the world through a different lens. That was the night my world was shit forever. A menace was born. A demon who denied the light.

"Hermano! Hermano! Come on, what are you doing?" Lethal's voice rings inside my eardrums.

"Yeah, wassup with the bait man?"

A blaze of fire flashing over my head, blinds my eyes.

"Man you know what's up," I look at Lethal, "why you bring other people to this private job?"

Unmoved by what I have to say, Lethal and I are hovering over each other in the back of a cold wet warehouse. I know he had people searching the city for Drew, but I do not under any circumstance want this to get out to anybody. I especially don't want to be implicated if either one of these niggahs are soft. They standing across from us waving around that damn blow torch like they're having the time of their lives. This is a man's job and the way I'm about to fuck this man up is going to be unforgettable.

"Ay, take the tape off of his mouth." Lethal tells the tall dude. "He looks like he isn't breathing."

He replies, "but boss I thought we was ending dude anyway."

"Do what I say." Lethal says.

With all the bullshit I got going on in my life I haven't had a chance to even think about this scene. Finally getting to face the muthafucka who's been turning my life upside down for months. Fucking my workers, pillow talking to bitches, a part of me knows why, but I want to hear it out of his mouth.

The way they have him tied down to the chair is some ol' foreign shit. All hemmed up with a blindfold and mouth cover tied together. I would hate to be him right now.

Even years later he looks the same besides those wack ass baby locs he ain't gone get a chance to grow out.

The smaller dude says to the taller guy, "aye Spaz wake this punk up."

Spaz takes a bucket of water on the ground next to his feet and splashes it in Drew's face.

"Huh!" Both of Drew's eyes shoot wide open. "What?!"

We lock eyes. *My niggah Drew.* The same hood niggah who I used to roll with tough. If you think about it, it's crazy how life turns on you. One minute you riding with yo' partners for life, the next you planning out how you gonna dig their grave. I always knew I was the smartest out of all the homies in the hood. Then again when I brought them in it I wanted out. Their problem was that they fell in love with the game. I always remembered the second I bussed my first cap in my own girl's dome, I got hold of the truth...there ain't no real love in the streets.

"Mhm," grumbling his throat, "so you sent these lil niggahs to flood my hide out, huh?" He looks at me then Lethal, "you and this mixed breed cocksucker."

162

"Oh," I laugh, "look like you the only niggah I know out here sucking dick."

Drew spits out some blood on the ground, "man niggah fuck you!" He shouts out.

"You ain't ever been a real niggah anyways."

Lethal adds in, "and you ain't never been a real man, punta!"

The rage exploding in my mind wants to blow this man's brains back right here, right now. With court in a few hours I don't have no time to waste. Either he gone say what he mean, mean what he say, or ain't gonna have nothing else to say again.

"So what's the problem then niggah?" I ask him, "you track me all the way to another state and instead of coming at me like a man you spread rumors like the little bitch you are."

Taking my jacket off I roll up the sleeves on my suit.

"I ain't gotta tell yo' pussy ass shit niggah!" Drew yells, "you just better kill me now."

I hand my jacket to the dude Spaz standing next to Lethal.

"Do I look like a bus boy niggah?" He asks.

Bop! Bop!

Jabbing him in the face then stomach he drops down to his knees.

I see his friend approaching me in the corner of my eye.

"Aye niggah!" He yells out.

I snatch the gun off Lethal's waist.

"I'll blow yo muthafuckin brains out lil niggah." I point the gun right at his temple.

I'm tired of muthafuckas playing with me ever since I turned over a new leaf. I will buss every niggah in this bitch. They better catch my fucking drift because I'm on whatever.

Lethal tugs on my arm, "Hermano! Hermano," he says, "calm down okay," snapping his fingers at the tall dude, "Snug... back up."

He replies, "but boss this niggah just..." "Back the fuck up! Now!" Lethal yells.

The lil' niggah takes a few steps back while his partner drags himself up off the floor.

One thing Lethal knows well about me is that when I get on that ass there's no regaining a peace of mind. He has his ways of doing his shit, now it's my turn to handle my business.

I look back at Drew, "yeah," I say, "so you was about to tell me why you decided to insert yo' pussy ass back in my fucking life."

The gloss in Drew's eyes is revealing all his deepest secrets to me. He ain't that same hot boy he used to be. As a matter of fact he never was about that life. Getting money, knocking off some hoes, and smoking weed is all he was ever about. I never admitted it to anyone out of the sake of the respect I had for him. Now? He can eat the metal piece of this bullet if he don't start talking.

A few seconds pass and he's still scanning every inch of the room to avoid the blank expression on my face.

Clack! Clack! Clack!

I crack the tip of the gun into his skull.

"Ahh! Fuck!" He yells out.

"So wassup niggah?!" I ask him, "I'm giving you the floor to speak so you better dance on that muthafucka!"

"Man," tears falling down his face, "I should've left you wandering the streets back then."

Clink! Clink! I cock back the trigger.

Pointing the gun at the center of his head, "fuck all that niggah!" Chewing on my lip, "speak up!"

At this point the way every niggah's face in here staring at me knows I ain't fucking around. This dude straight pussy! Sitting here damn near dead. And for what? I can throw apologies around all day for smoking his brother but that won't change the name of the game. The moment you step in you're never safe.

I shout out, "one, two," pressing on the trigger, "Say night night niggah."

"Okay! Okay!" Drew blurts out, "you took out my lover man!" He cries, "you shot my brother then you killed the niggah I was in love with."

Lethal speaks up, "aw man."

I drop the gun to my waist. Lost for words is the biggest understatement of the year. *His man?* First of all I made it very clear that I never gave one fuck about what another man does on his own time. How fucking ever, besides his brother, out of the three homies we took out that night it had to be out of Drop and the other dude Chris who nobody fucked with forreal.

Twisting the crook out of my neck, "wait a minute," clearing my throat, "you-you talking about the... you was smashing who, bro?"

Sniffling the air, "man don't judge me bro," he says, "we can't help who we love." "Bullshit." Spaz mumbles.

"So who was it bro?"

Sniffling on the snot dripping from his nose he mumbles, "Dr- Dr..."

"You was fucking with Drop dude?" I ask him.

"Well that explains all their late night outings," Lethal laughs.

Man this situation just got weirder. And now that I think about it he treated Drop like a store running pussyfoot who had to do everything he said. I can respect wanting revenge for his brother and all. But that explains his relationship with Tristian along with the relentless need to bring me down. I broke his heart.

The one question left is how did he find my location in the first place if Lethal's connected ass couldn't. He's working with someone close, and when I find out who that is, it's lights out for everybody involved.

I go on, "well since everything is out the only question left is how you found me?" I ask.

Drew panting out for air don't mean shit to me. Instead of him coming at me like a man he goes behind my back like a bitch. Fuck his pain.

Edging closer to him, "you got one time to beat around the bush with me, so I'd advise you choose your words wisely." I lower my voice.

He says, "I can't," he cries, "if I tell you they'll go after the only sister I have left."

I yank the chair.

"And if you don't tell me you're dead anyway so you better speak up."

"Ahh!" He yells out, "please Ace man why did it have to be like this man?"

The blood pumping inside my ears excludes any sorrow to have for this niggah.

"I understand," twisting on my watch, "I have time today, so I'll give you about 5 seconds before I blow yo muthafuckin head back niggah."

I flick the strap around in circles.

I start to count down, "5...4..."

"Okay! Okay." He says, "Pent," he sighs, "I was meeting with Pent, and I don't know how but he had all your information."

"Pent?" I ask, "that niggah dead!" I up the pole, "stop lying to me!"

"I'm for real bruh!" Drew yells back, "I met with him but it's the head of Drummer Boyz that really wants you."

"Who wants me? Duke?"

He may be right. I did so much dirt back then that I'm not surprised that that Opp ass coochie boy trying to get my head served on a silver platter. The thing is... I have no clue as to why he got smoke with me. I never inserted myself in any of his business.

"So that's it?" I ask him. "You linked up with a niggah who got smoked by one of Spider's people, now you up in this bitch about to reunite with yo' boyfriend."

Blinking the blood dripping from his forehead he sobs out in the air.

"Man," he says, "I told you everything I know... so please just let me go."

I get a glimpse of the small smirk on Lethal's face. There's no telling how long he's been waiting for this moment. I would let him take this niggah out himself but that'll leave me with the guilt of not doing it myself. Somewhere in my heart is wanting to let him walk out of here. After all we went through in the streets, including the drama connecting us. Then I think back to the amount of pain I'm in starting with his revenge plot.

He has nothing else to say meaning... he's dead weight.

"You know when I first got out of jail and you let me shack up with you and all those other niggahs I thought we was gone be boys for life..." staring him in his eyes, "then you sit up and stir up my life all because I had to protect myself," I say, "when you out of everybody I know understands how the streets work."

He blows out a breath, "you one of the smartest niggahs I know Ace," he says, "and you know the most important rule. At the end of the night you gotta make it back home. But when you lay yo' head down on that pillow tonight... I want you to remember that you'll never be nothing but a heartless niggah in a classy ass sui..."

Pop! Pop! Pop!

I squeeze three shots smacking him in the forehead. Blowing back blood and brains splattering all over my face.

"And you ain't never going home to yo' pillow." I say.

His body leans over in the chair.

"Boys," Lethal says, "clean this up."

Rushing to Drew's lifeless body Spaz and Snug start untying his hands from the chair.

I don't feel a thing. As a matter of fact I still have more business to get to before court starts. This night is going by fast as hell. I know Radiance is waiting on me at the house. I can't show up with a bunch of red stains all over my clothes, she'll ask too many questions.

"Hey," taking my shirt off, "burn these with the blow torch right quick," I say to Spaz."

With my jacket still in his hand I can feel him mean mugging me while I'm wiping the blood off my face into my button up.

I turn to him, "what lil niggah you still mad about that lil ruff up?" I ask.

"What bruh?!" He yells, "you better shut the fuck up talking to me... I ain't this ham ass niggah in the chair."

Both Lethal and Snug continue to take Drew's clothes off.

The one thing summing up this dude's fate is the next few words to come out of his mouth. He must've forgot I'm still clutching on this strap in my hand. I don't give one fuck about him being one of Lethal's workers or none of that.

"Mhm," I ease up to him, "I know you better respect yo' muthafuckin elders, young buck."

He sucks his teeth, "Pshh," stepping up to me, "you ain't bout that real life," he laughs, "you just a prissy boy."

With a smug smirk I take a quick look at Lethal then back to Spaz.

Cocking one bullet back in the chamber I clear it out right in the middle of this cake boy's skull.

Pop.

"Yo! What the fuck?!" Snug jumps up, "what did you do?!"

Spaz's body falls straight on his back.

"Hermano!" Lethal says, "perdiste tu puta cabeza!!" Running to my side, "crazy!"

I don't expect Snug's little ass to bust any moves, or he'll be next to get his ass dropped. And Lethal will be alright. I'm sure he didn't want to deal with a fuck niggah who ran his mouth too much anyways.

Coddling Spaz's head in his lap, Snug looks up at me.

"Bruh... he had a daughter," he says.

"She'll be better off," I reply.

He hops up on his feet.

"What you gonna do?" I stare him in the eye, "because if you take another step to me... you gone be lying next to both of them niggahs."

He takes a look at the bodies on the ground then backs up.

Lethal looks at me, "get out of here," he says.

I hand him back his gun then pick up my jacket off the ground.

"I'll have 1 million wired to you in the morning."

Ignoring the puddle of blood by our feet Lethal gets in my face.

"No," lowering his voice, "you will send two million to my account in the morning... brutha."

We hover over each other for the next few seconds. I see how it is. He's having a bitch fit about being short handed. As much power he has I'm sure he got another flunky lined up in every state to do his dirty work.

I smirk, "yeah okay," I say, "well I have things to do."

Heading out of the warehouse I hear Lethal's voice echo behind my back.

"Dingo." He says.

Throwing my jacket on, I tighten up the buttons as I fast walk down the street.

From what I know I'm 100 percent in the clear. Drew's taken care of, Keisha is going to give my office a W tomorrow, and I did it without a scratch. This shit you call life ain't easy but who said it was going to be. Everyone around me is starting to become a pawn in a game I thought I was done playing long ago.

Except, it's not the streets, it's the corporate world. If you take a minute to think about it you see it. A dog eats dog world. You either got money, power or clout and connections. Javeon runs the drug game, Lethal runs the hitman click, and I'm in the world of law. The main thing we have in common is we all have business to take care of. Whether it's dope to sell, a niggah to knock off, or a criminal to get out of jail. We run our own corporations. I just want to take a different route. After tonight I no longer want to catch any more bodies. When I first left my city behind I promised to live the life I always craved. That's to exist in my own universe with a loyal woman by my side. That means getting to the bottom of Radiance chopping it up with a random dude I've never seen before. I'm sure I may be overreacting, but you can never be too sure about every single thing these days.

I get back to my house with only a few hours to get a few z's in before court. *Damn.* Thinking to myself. I pause at the door to gather a good enough explanation for my long day of disappearance. *I was working late.* Nah, she probably went by the office. Or *I went by the water to clear my mind.* Shit, not that either... she'd probably assume I'm stressing about that bimbo broad. *Fuck it.* If I am going to be a pussy about the situation I should have one. Besides, she got more explaining to do than me about her day. It's fucked up but if anything I'll use that to get her off my ass.

I tap on my pockets and notice that I forgot my damn keys at the office earlier.

Knock. Knock.

I don't see any lights on, but her car is parked in the driveway, so she has to be here.

I knock again.

"Hey," she opens the door. "Where the fuck have you been?"

Pacing right past her I go straight to the bathroom in my bedroom.

"Devine!" Her little voice calls out on the other side of the door, "no call? No text? You had me worried sick all day."

Although I'm low key heated at her I have to get these clothes off of me first. She is going to be more pissed that I am ignoring her, but I can't think of the words to say.

Yelling from inside of the shower, "I'll be out in a minute." I reply.

I can feel her blood boiling on the other side of that door. Radiance is the calmest woman I know, so when she gets upset... she is pissed. But I'm a lawyer, I deal with pissed off people all the time. Then again, I don't stick pipe deep inside their guts either.

I hop out of the shower and throw a towel on before I open up the door.

"Babe, I need to talk to you about som..."

Chapter 15

One Way In; No Way Out

Stopping me in my tracks she's standing right at the door as soon as I pull it open.

"And you still haven't answered my question, Devine."

Walking past her again I flop down to the bed.

"And what's that?"

Playing dumb to throw her off is going to help me out in this situation a little bit. She's a very smart woman. There is no half stepping to her.

She comes to the bed.

"You know what," marching to her side, "I don't even care because I know you were probably with that bitch."

I knew it! On the other end of this I have to come up with something before she shuts down on me. And I be needing to feel her insides to sleep tight.

"I wasn't," I say, but there is something that threw me off. After my walk today I stopped by your shop."

She gets quiet so I go on.

"And I didn't see you... were you at home?"

She's laying on her side of the bed with her back facing me so I can't see the expression on her face. I can never tell what's going through this woman's skull and it drives me fucking crazy.

"Hello?" I ask, "why are you so quiet."

A few seconds pass and I start to hear her sniffling into the pillow.

"What's the matter baby?"

Pushing my stomach on her back, "what's wrong baby?" I ask again.

Wiping her cheeks, "I wanted to tell you for so long, but I was so scared of your reaction." She mumbles.

Two things... Either she's about to tell me she is cheating on me, or she is in some kind of trouble. Because the way her and dude was going back and forth I can tell he wanted something from her. If she needs any of my help she better speak up before I get mad.

"Talk to me baby," I say, "come here... look at me."

Rolling over I wipe the few tears dripping down her face with my fingertips.

"Well, when I left you I lived with my sister for a while... until I was able to get fully on my feet."

"Uh-huh," I reply.

"And it wasn't easy as you'd think a cheap town would be, but I got desperate after a while," she pauses, "and then that's when I met him."

"That's the guy you were talking to?"

Aww shit. Here comes the moment I've been waiting for. For her to tell me who this niggah is she been cheating on me with. I hope she don't say anything like that to me. My heart may break into pieces around this joint. And to be real, I have no idea how

I'm going to take that shit. If it comes down to it I'm gone force myself to be calm about it in every way possible.

Nodding her head, "he was so nice, gave me everything I wanted and then I got..." she sniffles again, "I had..."

Lifting up my back straightens against the headboard.

"You got... had what?" I ask.

Her eyelashes blink a hundred times every second she blows out a breath.

The blood rushing to my brain is blocking out any made up explanation for her. All I can do is wait on the next words to come out of her mouth.

"I have a kid!" She blurts out, "and the man you saw me talking to is friends with my babyfather."

In an instant I swallow a huge gulp of air.

"Oh-I... uhm, when? How old is he? She?"

Woah! I didn't expect her to have a tie to someone this deep. The most important question is why the hell she wait this long to tell me about her having a family. All those late night talks we had about starting our own. Something not sitting right about this situation. But I'm gonna hear her out.

"He is ten years old and Tyla isn't actually my blood, but he is still my son," she replies, "he's my step son."

"Oh, okay..." My head turns towards the TV, "So why is he having his friend come chop it up with you?"

I can respect her keeping in touch with her step son. I just hope she isn't about to tell me that she's married because that'll be a different story.

She sighs, "it's such a sensitive subject, but when I tell you I need you to not do anything reckless." She says.

"What do you mean?" I ask, "dude put his hands on you?! Are y'all still married? What?"

Patting my thigh, "no! No!" She shouts out, "it's just that..." her voice croaks, "I'm sorry but when I moved back here I tried to start over, and he found me and now he's holding Tyla over my head."

"Wait, wait, wait," I butt in, "slow down baby. You have to explain to me what you mean... so you ran away from dude, now he's holding the baby over your head? What do you mean by this?"

It is so important that I get to the bottom of this. From what I'm hearing she basically running from a niggah. And from my experience he either has some real money or got his hands deep in some kind of power. Enough to send a strong woman running for the hills.

"Well, I never really associated myself with his business, but I know for a fact he is very bad news... and I'm terrified of him Devine," tears burst out of both her eyes, "I can't live in fear. I just can't!"

Coddling her in my arms I squeeze tighter. I wanted her to feel my strong energy of never in life letting anyone fuck with her. I would say as long as I'm around regardless of that this shit between me and her is forever. I'm gone set up a hit on this niggah to get him out the way. She won't ever have to worry about this punk bitch again.

Taking a quick glance at the clock to see I have only two hours before court in the morning. I can't wait to get this over with. As soon as this man gets his plea deal I am taking my baby out of the country for however long she wants to get out of here. I'm saving it as a surprise though.

"I'm so sorry you are going through this baby," kissing her on the forehead, "but I promise I'm going to make it better, okay?"

She nods off in my arms a few minutes after. I assume she's exhausted from all the emotions setting in on her. I relate to her on many levels. Being lost in your own grief, wondering where life is about to take you. Fearful of your next moves. It gives me comfort that I can be that peace of mind for her. I'd give her the shirt off my back even if it was the only one I had left.

Pressing my lips to her forehead, "goodnight baby," I say.

The next morning I'm trying my best to contemplate why I woke up to one half of the bed empty. If I had time to search the city for her whereabouts I would. I'd rather be anywhere than standing in this courtroom surrounded by these delusional ass people.

Anxious about Keisha revealing her statements I play it cool to get this shit over with. I present my argument to the jury then she unveils hers. All the shit I am already aware of. The only thing left is her one and only witness that I'm sure I am about to break down on the stand after this final recess.

Javeon is laid back damn near slouching in his seat which means his balls less bunched up than usual. Keisha looking real tense with her fat fuck of a partner over there, signifying their early defeat. Everything is everything. Now, I can focus on finding out where my lady is.

"Aye so with ol' girl's shitty defense that only mean we good right," Javeon taps my leg.

With my head in my phone, "yeah," I whisper, "like we talked about this morning...they can't prove the RICO, but they can prove you in a gang so you're going to get at least a five year sentence for affiliation and that's it bro."

I sent for Tristian to send out a search for her, he hasn't got back with any information yet. If I could walk out this muthafucka right now I would. I'm running out of here as soon as the jury reads the verdict.

In the middle of recess almost being over my phone vibrates. I almost shit myself when I see an unknown number pop up across the screen. *Who is this?* I step out of the courtroom to pick up the call.

"Hello?" I answer.

A stubborn voice clears their throat before saying anything.

"Hey, Mr. Staxx it's Sam!" She says.

"Oh hey," I reply, "I didn't know you were back at work. How are you?"

"Fine, fine," she says, "but I want to get straight into it because I am a little backed up," she goes on, "well, I got your request about a deep background on a Roshaun Cole, and we didn't have much at first seeing that he seems to have gone off the grid almost 10 years ago."

My day is just getting better than ever. Who would think that I'll have even more of an upper hand on Keisha's 'secret' witness right before he takes the stand. I don't see it any other way than a major win on my end. Life is crazy as hell. You rumble through a bunch of twists and turns to get to the finish line. In the end everything turns out to be alright.

"Oh," I say, "well I'm sure he didn't go anywhere too far."

Sometimes things never add up. I start to think that if the prosecution's been building a case on Javeon for that long besides Keisha's and I deal to throw the case, why is the evidence they had on him so shitty. When you connect the dots you see that they really just throw a lot of nothing together to make it out to push whatever narrative they want it to be.

"I assure you it gets deeper than that Mr. Staxx... you are familiar with the 422-143-Request to Change Sex Designation on a Birth Certificate?" She asks.

"Uhm, I don't think I am."

I'm a little conflicted with where she's going with this conversation. I do know almost every law in every state, but I never got deep into the gender laws. The only thing I know is that it became legal to change it in the mid-1800's.

"Well that's okay I'll explain, the Gender Recognition Act provides a process for individuals to amend their gender designation on state-issued identification documents."

Peeking through the doors I see Judge Rowling taking his seat at his bench.

"Okay," I cut in, "so this person changed their gender... Did you find any information deeper than this."

I hear her fingers clicking on her computer mouse.

"Yes of course," she replies, "I found in Roshaun's juvenile record a bunch of petty theft charges... all the way up to his request to change his gender marker from male to female."

When he changed his gender from male to female he must have decided to keep his name Roshaun Cole? But this dude slick as hell to not be found by Javeon's soldiers testifying without witness protection on a major case can put anyone in danger going up against a niggah like Javeon. He must be rolling out soon as he testifies.

"Great, I can use this to my advantage for the witness' credibility thank you," I ask, "one last question I have though... what is the name 'she' identifies by?"

If I can count on anybody I'd always put my money on Sam to get the job done. This walk in the park feels more like a walk up the stairs to heaven. I can already smell the aroma of hate oozing from Keisha's energy.

Taking a few more seconds I ease towards the door to see if anybody's movement has changed but nothing has.

She says, "I thought I pinned the note of her name... it's somewhere in here."

"It's okay if you don't, I have enough in..."

"Here it is!" She cuts in, "the name registered here in the system is Radiance Strodem."

"What the fuck did you just say?!" I shout out... "I mean can you repeat that for me please?"

When I tell you my stomach is about to drop to the fucking floor. Then what do you know! This bitch is being escorted out to the stand.

"Are you okay Sir?" She repeats, "I said Radiance Strodem born, February 15, 1989."

I instantly hang up the phone when all the words she was saying began to slur together. I can't do none of this shit! What the fuck is... Why the fuck? *Aww man!* I have never been this mad in my fucking life. The ground under my feet is shaking. Radiance? A trans...a fucking transgender! How could she do this to me?! For over ten years she lied to my face, not even giving me a chance to decide on how I want to live my life. That niggah Drew was right you can't help who you love. At the same time you have to get to the true colors of the people you decide to lay down with.

I have to take the blame on this one.

I also have five seconds to pull my shit together by the time I'm face to face with her.

This shit has rocked me to my fucking core.

Going through the doors I turn a blind eye to the small smirk on Keisha's face. She's hovering in front of Radiance holding that same picture of that dude Pent that Javeon allegedly took out.

Both these hoes played a good game for sure. Acting foreign to each other in my office. Keisha showing her ass to throw me off while Radiance fake loving ass shows me a good time. The one time I let my emotions overtake my rational mind I take three upper cuts to the dome.

"You good bro?" Javeon whispers to me.

I nod back without saying a word.

I don't have the energy for any extra conflict right now. My soul is in shambles along with all the mixed emotions of how I'm about to tear this bitch up on the stand and in real life.

Looking at me, "Nice of you to join us Mr. Staxx," he says then points back at Keisha, "your floor Miss Turner," Judge Rowling says.

"Yes your Honor," she says, "now Shawn Knowles, also known as Pent, was a part of the Hotboyz Drug Corporation," staring at Radiance, "meaning he ran drugs for them before he was taken out, correct?"

Considering the total blank look all over Radiance's face I can't stop the pain tearing a hole inside of my stomach. This is the most ridiculous scheme to mankind. Whole time I'm planning trips, life goals, kids. Kids! Whole time his hoe was playing in my face. And for what? She must've been fucking the dude Pent. It has to be that to get on the stand running her fucking mouth.

"Yes," Radiance replies.

"And you were at his house when he and another victim Amanda Bryant was indeed attacked by Javeon McCleaton, also known as Spider... the head of the Soundboyz Mafia?"

"Objection your Honor!" I speak up, "this new witness Amanda Bryant did not appear in the motion of discovery, being that the prosecution failed to disclose exculpatory evidence I'd like to highlight it is in indeed clear violation to the Brady rule."

Judge Rowling looks at Keisha, "approach the bench."

We head to the judge.

"Is this right Miss Turner?" He asks.

Keisha replies, "No, your Honor," she smirks, "it was actually in the second page of the discovery your Honor."

As she babbles to the judge I get a long glare at Radiance. She can't even look at me. But that's okay, cause when I get my turn I'm about to destroy her.

"Oh yes," Judge Rowling says, "here it is right here... it states that the witness here, Roshaun Cole, heard defendant Javeon McCleaton's voice after taking out both victims, then saw him give an order to another man," looking at me, "did you miss this when you looked over it or did you just not take a look?"

I can also take the blame for not seeing the other witness's name in the motion. Again, I don't give a fuck about none of that. It still don't justify how I'm about to give her what she looking for. At this point everyone can stop talking to me.

"Apologies to the court, your Honor," I say.

"Miss Turner will proceed with her witness." He says.

We both head back to our desks.

"Last question Radiance, who was the other witness Amanda Bryant to you?" She asks.

"My sister," Radiance sighs.

"Right, right," Keisha turns to the jury, "your sister..." looking at Radiance, "and you would indeed do anything for your sister by even risking your life to get justice for her, alongside the brutality that has taken a toll on her life. Correct?"

"Yes," she sighs, "I will do anything for the ones I love."

Oh this bitch is toast. I get it. She wants to defend her sister, so she fucked around in my space for months. I can care less about any of these bullshit excuses she's throwing out there to save her ass from the amount of wrath that's about to be unleashed, respectfully. We're about to see who gone get the last laugh around this muthafucka.

"That is all," Keisha says, "your witness," she smiles at me.

I damn near jump out of my chair, "so Roshaun Cole," I say, "how old were you when you caught your first petty theft charge?" I ask.

Keisha's voice goes off behind my back... "Objection your Honor," she blurts, "relevance."

"Mr. Staxx," Judge Rowling says.

"Rule 611(c) " I reply. "Leading up to a point of connection your Honor." "Sustained," he replies.

"When I was a child, I hadn't been in any trouble in my adult years." She says.

I continue to grill her for at least two minutes about her past, from her childhood all the way to her adult years. I don't know why this broad let another weak link convince her she can get one up on me. There is never going to be a time where I don't get my lick back.

The jury is in awe on my side. I got her looking so bad that anything she can say to them isn't going to hold an ounce of weight. And I love it. This amount of stress has all kinds of veins popping out of her forehead. Fuck her. I want her to feel every inch of pain eating my soul up right now.

"Okay," tears start falling down her face, "I admit I hurt you!" She shouts out, "you're hurt... but that does not give you the right to try to humiliate me in front of all these people, Devine."

Brushing her off I turn to Judge Rowling, "that is all your Honor," I say.

I head back to my seat.

"But!" She yells out, "since we're airing things out I have one question. Does the jury know the real relationship between you and your client though?!"

Judge Rowling cuts in, "Miss Turner please quiet your witness."

Trying to keep my composure I give her a harsh look. The kind of stare that would kill if it had claws. There's no way she knows the ordeals between Javeon and me. I mean, I trusted her but something in me never allowed her in that deep. I don't have a single idea of what she's talking about right now.

Her face turns right to me then Javeon.

"Man, what this bitch talking about?" Javeon asks.

"So since I'm guessing you know the 'real' me now, right?" Radiance sniffles, "and everybody knows my business... so why don't you tell them yours huh?" She asks. "Why you don't you tell the court your client is actually your ain't shit long lost brother you told me about years ago?!"

"Huh!" Every face in the court turns up.

Ain't this about a bitch! My mind instantly checks out.

"Hey baby," Radiance asks, "how was your day?"

When we first met she would always come to my little ass apartment to chill and watch movies.

Sitting down at my desk studying for my finals, my phone vibrates.

Radiance looks at my screen, "well aren't you going to answer that?" She asks, "it may be important."

"Nah," I reply, "it's just my little brother calling about some legal advice... I'll get back to him later."

"Oh," what did you say his name was again?"

Throwing my books to the side I pull her body closer to mine.

"Javeon," I kiss on her neck, "we haven't been that close since my mom split us up when she left my dad though."

"Oh," she says, "I'm so sorry to hear that."

"It's no big deal," I say, "now come here so I can concentrate on giving you my world." We both laughed.

This shit is just about over. For the first time in my entire life I cannot find it in my heart to have a single solution. Only that I fucked up big time. I got through Javeon's shit, Lethal's bullshit, and even Keisha's bitching but I let my feelings get in the way. She got one up on me.

It all makes perfect sense now, my brother got her sister killed, now she's coming for the both of us. Can you blame her? I have always known to take full responsibility that's part of being a man...now I can only find myself on the other side of the sidewalk fighting for air outside of the courthouse.

Today is the most drastic day of my life. I'll never be able to get anyone's face out of my head when I stormed out of the courtroom. My head is in a daze, my stomach is full of shit that won't come up every time I hawk spit on the ground. I can't do this! *I'm going to kill both those bitches.* I feel more like a pussy for storming out of court. I can't see anything but Javeon's face after they called out the verdict.

Judge Rowling says, "The State of California versus Javeon McCleaton, we find the defendant guilty on all charges and sentenced to a maximum of 46 years to San Quentin State Prison."

"Man! Hell nah!' Javeon yells out. "Y'all don't know who y'all fucking with!"

"Guard please take the defendant out of my courtroom," Judge Rowling says "and Mr. Staxx I am very disappointed at your attempt to harbor your client's true relation in the court and I'm afraid I will have to send a copy of this record to the Bar Association. Now I can hold you in contempt of my court but since you have proved yourself a pillar I'll allow them to handle your case files, provided you are abiding by the law."

"Thank you, your Honor," I reply.

All these muthafuckas prayed for this day to see me fall. Right on my fucking face. And it was all because of a bitch.

Dun! Dun! Dun! Dun! Dun! Dun! Dun! Dun! Dun!

There's no telling who in the fuck is calling me. And I don't care, the only thing I know is I have to get home! I'm trembling through the alleyway I used to take when I walked to my old apartment.

Dun! Dun! Dun! Dun! Dun! Dun! Dun! Dun! Dun!

I look down to an unknown number going across my phone screen again.

"Hello!" I pick up the phone, "who the fuck is this!"

A hard voice laughs.

"So did you really think you was gone be able to fuck me over and live niggah?" I don't give a fuck about you being my momma son!" Javeon says. "You over with niggah!"

Fighting for some air, "man fuck you niggah!" I yell back.

Slamming my phone on the ground I go right with it.

"Fuck!" I scream at the air.

Next thing I hear is tires screeching towards me in the alley.

I hear a man's voice saying, 'grab him up' as my whole body shuts down. Then I pass out.

I wake up cold as fuck tied down to a chair.

"Huh?! What is this?!" I yell out, "get me the fuck out of here!"

I hear a trigger cock back then press against my temple.

I can't see anything but black. After a few minutes I decide to accept the fate of Javeon's last words to me. This is my last day on earth, I'm about to meet my Maker. A part of me is damn near relieved while the other half wants to fight to see who's on the other side of this blindfold.

"So you not gone at least show yo' pussy ass face!" I shout out.

A familiar voice starts to laugh loud as hell then snatches the blindfold off my eyes. I can't believe it! This must be the most betrayal I've witnessed in a decade. I shut my eyes to imagine me somewhere on the beach by my lonesome. Playing in the water by day, counting the stars at night. Before I open my eyes I blurt out the first thing that comes to mind.

"Oh so I see you still mad, huh?!"

Rule number 6 being a black man in America... Always be prepared for your past to come back and bite you in the ass because once you associate yourself in the streets, if you don't get smoked or drown inside of the prison system you in this shit forever. So do yourself a favor. And don't get comfortable niggah.

Devine

Devotions of a Boss

I pull up next to the building to see an all black Escalade in my parking spot.

What the fuck. Thinking to myself, this muthafucka has lost his mind. I'm going to do him a favor though. Keeping my cool is the best thing to do right now, especially with Lethal's fried ass on the phone.

Jumping out of my car I say, "aye bro I have to go but I hope you get everything figured out."

"So you just get to keep calling me to do you favors and I can't even get you to do this one cosa for me?"

"Look bro, I paid you for both jobs I needed done so don't act like you did me any favors when that's literally what you live to do."

What the fuck is he even still doing here?! For the last few months I've been regretting the shit out of that call I had to make to his ass. Deep down I knew he was going to become a major problem after everything had been done. He the same muthafucka he was when we were kids. And I don't want shit to do with him. Nothing at fucking all.

Walking inside the building I keep my eyes glued to my office, way in the fucking back of the building. Most times I have to ignore all the rattled stares I get from everyone, especially from the ones sitting at the computers. Some of the white folks amused, others still hold fear from my authority versus the brothers swearing that I sold out to the white man. I just keep my composure. That falls into Rule number 7 of being a black man in America, 'when yo balls hit the floor pick them muthafuckas back up and keep it pushing'. This life shit doesn't stop for nobody.

I get into the office then shut the door behind my back.

"Bro, look I just got into work and I have to go," I say to Lethal, "so I hope you can get everything figured out. I'll catch you on the rebound."

Click.

I have to bang on his ass before he gets to babbling that espanol shit like I understand what he's saying.

Made in the USA
Columbia, SC
18 June 2024

36918957R00117